A NEW ARRIVAL IN UPPER BAMTON

UPPER BAMTON BOOK 1

BETH RAIN

To Elspeth

All my love

Beth Rain

xxx.

CHAPTER 1

*A*lice Merryfield yawned as she bent to pull her trainers on, yanking at the laces to tighten them ready for a good, long run. She needed it this morning. She'd had enough of her brain tying itself up in knots. She'd been tossing and turning for most of the night, and she simply couldn't lie around any longer, even though the birds were only just starting to tune-up for their morning singsong. The sky was beginning to lighten outside her bedroom window and that was enough to tempt her out from under her duvet - even though she'd probably regret it later!

Heaving herself off the edge of her bed, Alice grabbed her fitness band from her dressing table and crept to the door. She opened it carefully. The last thing she wanted to do was disturb her father this early in the morning - otherwise he'd be like a bear with a sore head for the rest of the day.

Easing her way out onto the landing, Alice made her way slowly along the upstairs hallway of the old farmhouse, avoiding the loose floorboard as she went and hopping over the creaking step on her way down the stairs to the ground floor.

Padding across the smooth, age-worn flagstones, Alice pulled the back door open and breathed a sigh of relief as the cool air rushed in to greet her. She stepped outside and closed the door quietly behind her.

Alice hadn't bothered bringing her keys with her, there wasn't any point - they rarely bothered to lock up these days. Even if her dad did decide to randomly head out somewhere before she got back, Alice knew that the old spare key still hung on a hook under the bench out in his workshop - just as it had done since she was a little girl. Besides, if push came to shove, she could always clamber up the old apple tree outside her bedroom window and get in that way. She'd done that plenty of times when she'd been a teenager, after all!

Alice ambled away from the house and crossed onto the tussocky patch of grass that used to be a well-kept lawn. It badly needed cutting - just another job on what had become a never-ending to-do list. It felt a bit like nature was starting to creep up on them, but there never seemed to be enough hours in the day to beat it back again.

If Alice was being honest, it was as much as she and her father could do to keep the acres of vines tended and productive. Here at Upper Bamton Vineyard, business had to come first... but it did mean that their house, gardens, and the surrounding outbuildings had suffered over the years. It was all a bit rambling, overgrown and in need of some serious TLC.

Fighting down a wave of anxiety as a host of worries rose to assault her, Alice pulled one leg up behind her in a half-hearted stretch. It was time to run, time to clear her head and escape the nagging sense that she was about to drown in her own to-do list.

Bending from the waist in an attempt to stretch the sleep from her back and legs, Alice shook her arms out. She was now well past the point where running felt like a slow, early-morning torture session. She wasn't exactly a natural-born runner, but she'd come to love plodding around the countryside that surrounded Upper Bamton village and the vineyard. Usually, it felt like a bit of a luxury to grab half an hour for her run. Today, it was more of a necessity... that's if she didn't want to completely lose the plot before sundown.

Alice set off along the stony path that led away from the house. Following it around the corner, an old stone barn came into view and her panic went into overdrive. This was the current source of all her worries - it was in the middle of being converted into the vineyard's new visitors' centre - a project that she was *supposedly* in charge of.

Gah!

Putting on a burst of speed, Alice dashed past, doing her best not to look at it. It was such a shame that something she'd been so excited about to begin with had turned into such a disaster. But that's what you got for taking pity on your idiot ex-boyfriend and hiring him for the job, wasn't it?!

What she really needed to do was figure out a way to fix the mess she'd managed to land herself in... but that was what she'd been trying to do all night and it hadn't got her anywhere. So instead - she just needed a break from thinking about it altogether. Wishful thinking!

Usually, Alice loved nothing more than jogging around the acres of tended vines, or following the twisting, undulating curves of the river as it flowed along the lower borders of her home. She could run for hours without ever leaving the vineyard's boundaries if she wanted to - but today, she just *didn't* want to.

Making an executive decision, Alice turned her strides in the direction of the village instead. She felt the need to put a little bit of distance between herself and the root of her troubles - something that was pretty hard to do given that she quite literally lived, worked and breathed the vineyard. She couldn't really imagine life any other way, but it meant that there was no respite from her worries.

Every day, Alice was surrounded by the rolling Devon hillsides where their precious vines flourished on the slopes that led down to the banks of the river Bamton. Yes, it was idyllic. Yes, it was a *total* headache.

It had been a long time since she'd just relaxed and

enjoyed the home she loved so much. In theory, it should be heaven living here. In reality, it had become a daily reminder of how much work there was to be done.

It hadn't always been that way, though. The vineyard had been the most amazing place to grow up. She'd adored the freedom of running wild, playing on rainy days in the dilapidated old boathouse down by the water's edge. On sunny days, she'd swum in the gentle bends of the river – floating along on her back while staring up at the forget-me-not patches of sky peeking through the dancing green leaves of the oaks that stretched their boughs out from the banks.

Even though Alice had lost her lovely mum when she was little, her childhood had been perfect - her father had made sure of that. It had just been the pair of them ever since - and it had never dawned on her as a kid that her dad's insistence on keeping the world at bay might be in the least bit odd. All his fences, gates and signs designed to keep unwanted visitors out had just been something he did to keep her safe - to keep their home safe. They had a few carefully chosen friends, and other than that it was the two of them against the world. It still was.

As the wide swell of the river appeared before her, Alice did her best to let the sound of the water wash the tension from her shoulders. It was proving more difficult than usual this morning – but that wasn't really surprising, was it?

It was no good. No matter how hard she tried to lose herself in happy memories, her problems just kept bobbing to the surface...

The visitors' centre. What on earth was she going to do about the visitors' centre?!

It had taken Alice long enough to convince her father that they needed to put some plans in place to revitalise the vineyard - months and months of cajoling, nudging, suggesting and bullying. Eventually, after the success of her trial-run Christmas party that she'd hosted in the winery itself – he'd grudgingly admitted that she might have a point. They needed to attract new customers if they were to survive, and to do that, they needed to let people back into their world. At long last, he agreed that she could make a start on the visitors' centre.

Alice's grand plan was to turn the old stone barn into a warm and cosy space where they could welcome the local community back to the vineyard after so many years of being shut out. She'd decided to start with a wine and wool evening. It had seemed like such an easy, simple way to get everyone together. All they'd need was a bunch of chairs, some tea, coffee, biscuits and, of course, plenty of wine for tasting!

The very first *Knit One Pour One* was due to happen in just over a week, and everyone was so excited about it. She couldn't believe she was going to have to let them all down!

Upper Bamton didn't have a space for the community to gather in anymore. The old village hall had fallen into disrepair years ago and there simply wasn't the money lying around to restore it. No doubt it would be sold off to some developer and turned into a holiday home before too long.

It was happening more and more around the area. Slowly but surely, communities were beginning to wither. It didn't help that so many of the old houses were being bought up as second homes and often sat empty for most of the time – playing host to their rich owners just once or twice a year when the fancy took them.

That was definitely a positive thing that had come from her father being so protective of their land at the vineyard. Sure, Arthur Merryfield may have driven the locals away with all his gates and fences. And yes, maybe the hundreds of signs warning off trespassers - and the fact that he discouraged visitors of any sort - was a bit of a nightmare when it came to building a reputation for their wines. But Arthur had taken the same hard-line approach when it came to developers too. This had safeguarded their land over the years. He could have sold off parcels of it a thousand times over – especially the bits with the beautiful stone buildings.

Alice eyeballed the boathouse as it loomed ahead of her down the path. This gorgeous old timber-framed building was a prime example. Her father could have made a fortune by selling it off along with the little bit of riverside land that surrounded it. Her dad might have many faults – but Alice was grateful that he'd guarded their home with such ferocity.

She adored the boathouse. Sure, it needed a lot of work – just like the rest of the place – but there was something magical about it. Sitting right at the edge of the river, it was always filled with the sound of rushing water. Alice always thought that it was the perfect place to mark the seasons with all her senses – surrounded as it was by bluebells in the spring and old oaks that, in autumn, dropped their golden leaves into the swirling eddies of the river.

Alice had always rather fancied living in the boathouse herself one day, but with one thing and another she'd never actually managed to make the move. It wasn't so bad remaining in her family home – but... well... sometimes she couldn't help but feel a tiny prickle of regret that she hadn't spread her wings a bit more when she was younger. She'd never travelled. Never left the vineyard. But then - she'd never wanted to leave her dad. There wasn't really any chance of that now - she was needed here – especially with the mess she'd managed to land them in.

Not that she wanted to leave... not really... but still, it might be nice to have a space she could call her own - even if it was just down the path near the river!

Alice put on a burst of speed and flew past the boathouse. She sprinted down the path that led towards the old stone bridge right at the edge of their land. From there, she could make her way over into the village itself.

What she needed now was a solution. She had a half-finished visitors' centre that looked worse than it had done before the work started, a bunch of eager knitters ready to descend in less than two weeks, and all her plans for revitalising the vineyard felt like they were in tatters.

Alice's little sprint had proved more than her lungs could take and she paused for a moment, resting her hands on her thighs as she tried to catch her breath.

What the hell had she been thinking, giving Warren and his team of builders the job? Actually, she knew exactly what she'd been thinking... or in this case, *feeling*. She'd been feeling guilty for dumping him. She was such an idiot! After all - she'd dumped him for a good reason... and he'd shown her his true colours once again, hadn't he?

The entire team had dropped her like a hot stone when another, more profitable job had come up. One day they simply stopped turning up. She still couldn't believe that they'd just disappeared and left her in the lurch!

Urgh. Just the thought of Warren made her shoulders tighten up around her ears again. The thing that made matters even worse was that she'd vouched for him with her dad, too. He'd warned her that she might be making a mistake, but she'd not listened.

Alice let out a great puff of air and straightened up.

It was time to get moving again. Dwelling on the fact that Warren had buggered off wasn't going to help her solve her problems, was it? She needed to run through her options again.

She'd already contacted Sam over in Little Bamton to ask if he might be able to help, but his award-winning cabin business was doing so well that he was booked solid for months. He was a lovely bloke and had offered to give up his week of holiday in August to come and help her out – but that would be far too late for the *Knit One Pour One* event.

Alice tried to match her breathing to her pace, but the knot of nerves in her stomach was making it practically impossible. It didn't help that she'd just realised that there were about a hundred posters for the event optimistically attached to her favourite gateposts and fences all around the village. She'd have to come out again later on and take them all down. It was time to face facts - she had nowhere suitable to hold it so she was going to have to cancel.

The winery was too big and not at all comfortable for this kind of event. The boathouse was full of junk, the workshop was full of random odds and ends of machinery, and their house - although comfortable and homey - was a bit of a pigsty.

As she rounded a bend in the riverside path, Alice stared ahead at the old stone bridge that would carry her over the vineyard boundary and into the village. She stopped in her tracks and let out an indignant huff.

There was a scruffy old green van parked up just before the bridge next to the river. On vineyard property.

'Bloody cheek!' she muttered.

It had been a favoured spot for camping before her father had put up signs all around the little pull-in. Clearly, this unwanted visitor didn't give two hoots though. Well, she'd see about that.

Alice strode towards the parked vehicle, determined to send them packing. As she neared, she cocked her head slightly.

What on earth?

Coming to a standstill right next to the van, she realised that the strange sound that had caught her attention was coming from somewhere inside. She put her ear close to the dusty green side and listened.

Snoring! There was someone inside the van snoring their head off. Seriously?! This *wasn't* a camping spot. It was private land. It wasn't for parking-up – and it *definitely* wasn't for sleeping in! Weren't the signs clear enough? After all, there *were* six of them!

Alice couldn't help but smirk – that was *so* like her father. Why use one sign when you could have six? Still, they hadn't worked, had they? Not when there was some random stranger catching up on their beauty sleep less than a few feet away from the warnings!

Alice sighed. She still had several miles of her run to go – and she didn't particularly fancy spoiling it by having an argument with whoever was making all that racket. She was in a bad enough mood as it was.

It was such a lovely morning, and she was already risking ruining her run by thinking about Warren – an argument with a random stranger would definitely tip her over the edge.

Nope – she'd keep going. She'd take the long loop through the village. Then she'd head back to the farm-house and grab some breakfast. Maybe the van would be gone by the time she had the chance to come back. Besides, she'd need to come this way again later to take all her posters down.

Alice let out a sigh. Gloom settled on her shoulders again as she jogged away from the van and the snoring visitor.

CHAPTER 2

*C*oming to a halt outside the back door, Alice checked her wristband. Hm – considering that she'd stopped a couple of times and lost several minutes listening to the rumbling snores emanating from the van down by the bridge, it wasn't a bad time at all. In fact, she'd hazard a guess that she might have even clocked up another record if it hadn't been for the interruptions.

She grinned and gave herself a mental pat on the back. Right – enough of all that, it was time to hot-foot it upstairs for a shower and then join her dad for breakfast.

Letting herself in, she decided that perhaps it'd be better not to mention the trespasser to him – at least, not yet. He was never really in the best frame of mind until he'd had his fifth coffee of the day, and he was already a bit more grouchy than usual with the various changes she was trying to put in place. Her dad might agree with her in principle that it was time to open their doors to the outside world again, but the reality of it was another thing entirely.

Alice took the stairs two at a time. Shower. Breakfast. Then she'd nip back down to the bridge herself and deal with their unwanted guest. If she dealt with it *before* telling her dad, that would at least make things a tiny bit better.

Ten minutes later, after a speedy shower, Alice wandered into the farmhouse kitchen having been led back downstairs by the enticing scent of what was probably her father's second cafetière of the day.

'Morning, sunshine!' said her dad, the minute she stepped through the door.

'Any left for me?' said Alice, nodding at the cafetière before heading over to him and dropping a kiss on his head. She rounded the table and plopped down into the empty chair across from him.

'Of course!' he said with a grin. 'I saw you pelting back up the path ten minutes ago, so I put the kettle on for a fresh pot!'

'My hero!' said Alice, doing her best not to dribble as her dad poured coffee into her favourite earthenware mug that was a bit like a bucket. 'Thank you!' she said gratefully as he handed it across the table to her, followed by the milk jug.

'Good run?' he asked, picking up a thick slice of

golden toast smothered in strawberry jam and taking a whopping bite.

'It's nice out there,' said Alice with a nod.

'But...?' her dad prompted with his eyebrows raised.

Damn. He really didn't miss a trick, did he?

'But... I've got a lot on my mind, and it kept getting in the way of actually enjoying it,' said Alice with a sigh.

Arthur nodded. 'Well, yes. It's not brilliant that you've been left in the lurch like this, I have to say.'

Uh oh. She needed to head this off at the pass before her dad decided to start questioning all their plans. Again. Time to downplay things and get them feeling upbeat asap.

'It's fine!' said Alice, forcing a cheery grin. 'I've still got a few leads to chase up yet.'

She paused and took a swig of coffee. She had no idea how convincing she sounded, but she really needed her dad to believe in her plans right now.

'So, do you reckon you can get your knitting club up and running in spite of everything?' he asked, raising his eyebrows.

Alice nodded, shooting him a bright smile that was the complete opposite of how she was really feeling.

'That's good news,' said Arthur. 'It would be a real shame if you had to cancel because my old friend from Seabury is planning on coming along. You remember Lionel?'

'Of course I do!' laughed Alice.

Her dad always introduced Lionel into conversations like this... *my old friend from Seabury... you remember Lionel?* In actual fact, Lionel had been a family friend forever. A little bit eccentric, always kind, there had never been a time when her father's old friend hadn't been part of their lives.

'He knitted both my favourite jumpers,' she added. 'He was here... what... just a couple of months ago for more wine? Besides... who could forget Lionel once they'd met him?'

'You have a point,' said her father with a grin. 'Well, he loved the idea of *Knit One Pour One* when I first mentioned it and he keeps asking me when it's going to happen. Anyway - I gave him the date and he's going to drive up for it.'

'Well... that's nice!' said Alice, secretly wondering what the hell she was doing. Hadn't she *just* decided on her run that it was time to throw in the towel and cancel the event? But here she was, telling her dad the exact opposite.

'He bought The Pebble Street Hotel, you know,' said Arthur, chomping on the last mouthful of toast before licking a blob of jam off of his thumb.

Alice nodded. 'I know.'

'He's been buying our wine for years, but I expect he'll be ordering quite a bit more as soon as he gets those visitors piling into Pebble Street. He's considering using us exclusively!'

'That's brilliant!' said Alice. Because it was brilliant. The whole point of opening the vineyard back up to the public and fostering relationships with their local community was to build up their brand name and increase their sales. After all, this was a massive place, and it was high time that it started to pay for itself. Yes – a hotel that exclusively served their wine would be a massive boon… so why did she suddenly feel more stressed than ever?

'So, you'll keep me up to date with the details for *Knit One Pour One* won't you?' prompted her father.

'Of course,' said Alice, her voice tight and scratchy. Where the *hell* was she going to host all these knitters?

She focused on buttering a piece of toast as she let her mind wander over the possibilities for the umpteenth time. Maybe they could use the winery just this once. After all, they'd held the huge Christmas party in there and that had been a great success. The vast stainless-steel vats and old barrels had provided the perfect backdrop to the large, round tables and groups of rowdy revellers.

But no - this was different. It simply wouldn't work. The winery was way too big. It was grand and cavernous… she wanted warm, welcoming and cosy. Now that she knew Lionel would be there too, the pressure was definitely on. There was no way she could cancel now. She *had* to find some sort of solution.

Alice glanced across at her father who was busily buttering another slice of toast, and she couldn't help but smile. He might not be wholly comfortable with the changes she was pushing for, but at least he wasn't giving her a hard time about hiring an ex-boyfriend to do the work. Arthur would have been well within his rights to hold her responsible for the current disaster they were dealing with, but he hadn't made her feel like it was her fault for a single second. It was something she was incredibly grateful for. Her dad had never liked Warren… and now she could see why.

'Where are you off to again in such a hurry?' he demanded as Alice practically leapt to her feet.

'Lots to do!' she said, forcing a grin onto her face and picking up a piece of toast to take with her. 'Thanks for the coffee!'

Arthur shrugged and started pouring himself another cup. 'You'll get hiccups, you know!'

Alice waved as his parting words followed her out into the hallway. As much as she'd love to sit in the kitchen for hours chatting with her dad, the knowledge that some random stranger was currently taking a nap down by the bridge was starting to bug her. It was time to go and check if he was still there. Besides – it would be the perfect opportunity to take some of her frustration out on their unsuspecting, unwelcome visitor.

It was turning into an absolutely beautiful day, and as she strode along the path back down towards the river, the cheerful fringes of pink campion and cow parsley fluttered in the light breeze. The trees overhead were thick with sappy leaves and everything felt rich and alive.

Alice took in a deep gulp of sweet air and let it soothe her - or at least, as much as it could as she marched along, getting ready for a fight. Even at this distance, she could see that the van hadn't moved off while she'd been eating her breakfast.

Well, that was just fine. Clearly, it was going to be one of *those* days. Alice felt her mood darken until she was like a little thundercloud stomping down the flower-lined path.

Reaching the van, she marched straight up to it and peered through the driver's window, cupping her hands against the glass. There was no one in there. Perhaps they were still asleep in the back. She drew away, wondering how best to go about this. Maybe she should knock on the back doors?

Come on Alice, man up!

She was just about to stomp around the back of the van when a loud sploshing sound caught her attention, and she turned towards the river, peering down the bank.

Oh. Blimey. There was someone down there. A man. A very naked man by the looks of things. Now that was something you didn't see every day!

The stranger was up to his waist in the river and didn't seem to have noticed her. Alice bit her lip, staring. What should she do? Come back again later? Wait up here until he was done?

Nope, sod that. She just needed to get his attention. 'Hello?'

It was a pathetic attempt - a punky, quiet croak. Alice had to give herself a little shake. For goodness sake, she needed to get a grip!

'Hello?!' she shouted. There. That was better. Nice and clear... and a little grouchy.

The guy's head turned briefly in her direction, and he shot her a grin. Cheeky blighter!

'Be right with you!' he called back.

Alice's jaw went slack as he promptly disappeared from sight, submerging himself completely under the water. She watched the patch of river where he'd disappeared with growing unease. He'd been under for what seemed like ages already. Like... a *really* long time.

Damn it, if he didn't come up again soon, she was going to have to bloody well dive in after him and save him, wasn't she?

Alice took a couple of tentative steps down the bank, busily planning which items of clothing she should take off first and where she could pile them – when he reappeared in a rush of water and sunlight.

She came to a total standstill, staring hard. The guy had short, dark hair that was glistening with droplets, and muscles where she'd never seen muscles before. And yup – he was *definitely* naked.

'Would you mind throwing me my towel?' he called.

Alice couldn't move. She just stood and stared, completely spellbound.

'It's just there?' he said, gesturing towards the bank below her.

'Oh, yeah... right, okay!' said Alice, snapping out of her trance and hastily stumbling towards the towel before bundling it into a ball and flinging it at him.

'Cheers!' he grinned, catching it easily.

Alice quickly turned her back to give him a chance to climb out onto the bank without being thoroughly ogled. She could feel her face radiating heat as she listened to him sloshing out of the river behind her. She was doing her best not to track his every move in her mind's eye, but it was proving difficult. Okay... impossible.

Floundering around trying to get a grip on herself, Alice remembered that she was meant to be cross with this bloke. After all, he was a trespasser, wasn't he?! In fact – it suited her right now to be angry with him... at least that might help her get over the whole *naked in the river* thing.

'Okay, you're safe.'

The guy's deep voice shook her from her trance, and she spun around to face him again. Thankfully, he was now dressed in a tatty old pair of board shorts and a grungy green tee shirt. Best not to look at him too long though – she was sure she could still see the outline of those muscles through the soft cotton.

'You're camping on private property,' she said, her voice coming out in a stroppy hiss as she crossed her arms over her chest.

'No, I'm not,' he said mildly, pulling on a grubby trainer.

'I heard you snoring earlier!' she said.

'That wasn't me,' said the guy, peeping up at her briefly before turning his attention back to his laces.

'Don't be ridiculous,' huffed Alice.

'I wasn't – that was Basil.'

'Who's Basil?' demanded Alice with a raised eyebrow.

'Come with me and you can meet him,' said the stranger. 'Oh, I'm Jake, by the way,' he added as he trudged past her and made his way up the bank, back towards the van.

Alice had no choice but to follow him, doing her best to keep her eyes off the nicely firm bum just in front of her.

'I'm Alice,' she muttered, remembering her manners as she picked her way through the undergrowth.

They'd just reached the top of the bank when Alice spotted a seriously grumpy looking dog trotting towards them from the direction of the van. He had a bent nose, little piggy eyes and was built like a tank.

On spotting the pair of them, the bull terrier paused in his tracks, stretched and gave a gigantic yawn. Then he peered at Alice with a definite hint of suspicion.

Alice paused, watching him warily.

'Basil's alright,' laughed Jake.

Alice nodded, not taking her eyes off the little dog as he stared at her hard. After a couple of seconds, he clearly decided that she'd passed some kind of top-secret canine test because he started to wag his tail.

Even though he still looked decidedly grumpy, Basil trotted over to her and leant his considerable weight against her leg, demanding a tickle.

'Okay – colour me officially impressed,' laughed Jake, watching as Alice gingerly stroked the dog's head. 'That doesn't happen very often – Basil can be a surly little so-and-so and won't accept tickles from just anyone. Looks like he's taken a shine to you, though!'

Alice glanced up at Jake, doing her best to wipe the soppy smile from her face. Piggy eyes and bent nose be damned - it was love at first sight!

'Look,' sighed Jake, 'I'm not camping. I'm afraid we broke down and I just about managed to steer the old girl across the bridge out of the way before she ground to a halt. It was really late last night, and we'd just driven all the way down from Scotland. It was pitch dark and I was completely wiped out. I didn't see the signs until this morning.'

Alice felt the knot of anger she'd been nurturing all morning starting to loosen slightly.

'Seriously,' said Jake, watching her, 'I didn't mean to cause any trouble. We'll be gone as soon as I can figure out what's gone wrong with the engine this time. She's seen better days I'm afraid! If I can't fix her myself, I might need to find someone with a tractor to tow me out of your way – I can always do a few hours of work in return for the help.'

As he'd been talking, Jake had made his way around the back of the van. He opened the doors and flung his damp towel inside. Alice could see that it was full of all sorts of tools as well as what looked like most of his worldly possessions and a pile of bedding. This was clearly more than just his way of travelling from a to b.

'What sort of work do you do?' she asked, curiously.

'I can turn my hand to most things,' said Jake with a shrug. 'I just spent several months helping someone to restore an old stone house on a tiny Scottish island – a place called Crumcarey? You probably won't have heard of it, not many people have. Before that I travelled all over Ireland and then Europe, working on different buildings... what?!' Jake paused, looking at her with a slightly alarmed expression.

Alice couldn't blame him. It was like the dark clouds that had been threatening to overwhelm her had just parted and a little ray of sunlight had broken through. He probably thought she was a complete lunatic - going from super-grouch to grinning idiot in a matter of seconds. She couldn't help it though - at long last, things might just be looking up. Had the universe really just dropped the solution to her problems right into her lap?

'You know,' she said slowly, 'you might be just the person I've been looking for!'

CHAPTER 3

*A*lice peered towards the house, trying to gauge where her father might have got to in his morning routine. The lights were still on in the kitchen window, so with any luck, he'd be working his way through yet another cup of coffee. It *might* just give her enough time to sneak around to the barn and grab the tractor before he figured out she was up to something.

Of course, he'd hear it as soon as she fired up the engine - and she'd have to pass the house on her way back down to the bridge. Even so, this was one of those things she'd prefer to explain *after* she'd done it rather than clear it with her dad first.

Ducking her head, she scurried along the stony, side path that they barely ever used because it got ridiculously slippery whenever it was wet. This morning, however, it was probably her safest route as it wasn't overlooked by any of the farmhouse's main windows.

As soon as she reached the wooden doors of the barn, she unbolted them and hauled them open, making as little sound as possible. There she was – their gorgeous tractor. The one thing in this place that was well maintained and looked after.

Alice promptly clambered up into the seat and turned the key. The tractor rumbled to life beneath her. She loved driving it – after all, she'd learned to drive in one. Not this one, but the old Massey Fergusson that was sitting in a rusty heap at the far end of the orchard. It was one of her dearest wishes to cut back the dome of brambles that had grown over its rusty form and restore it to its former glory. Unfortunately, there were so many other things that needed her attention around this place, the old tractor didn't rank very highly on her list of priorities.

Turning her attention back to the job in hand, Alice put the tractor in gear and slowly eased her way out of the barn. She turned onto the wide sweep of rocky track that would lead her through the yard and down towards the bridge.

She loved the different view that sitting high up in the tractor's seat offered her. It was always nice to see the vineyard from a different angle – it helped her to remember just how magical the place was. Right... it was time to get started on her rescue mission.

Alice considered what Jake had told her so far.

Maybe he *could* help with her current emergency – though whether he would *want to* was another matter entirely. Still, she was more than willing to give his van a tow away from the river in return for a quick chat about the visitors' centre. Maybe a fresh perspective on the project might help her to spot some options that she hadn't considered yet.

'Dad?!' Alice drew the tractor to a halt as her father appeared in front of her on the path. Damn – she'd really hoped to find out a bit more about Jake before explaining what was going on to her father. He could just be so cantankerous sometimes, and she didn't want him to scare Jake off!

Alice could see that her dad was trying to ask her a question. Even though she couldn't hear him over the rumbling vibrations of the tractor, she could tell by his body language that he wanted to know what on earth she was up to. Of course, the adult thing to do would be to hop down and explain what was going on, but for some reason, a rebellious, teenage side of her took over.

'Sorry, can't hear you!' she singsonged, cupping her hand behind her ear and grinning at her dad. She saw him roll his eyes and gesture for her to get down and explain.

Alice couldn't help but giggle. She'd seen that eye roll so many times when she'd been growing up, and a warm wave of affection hit her. Still – she was determined to do this thing *first and* then explain later.

'Later!' she bellowed. Then mouthed the word again, slowly so that he could see what she was saying.

Her dad, clearly deciding that she must have lost the plot and was best left to get on with it, shook his head in exasperation and turned away. Alice watched as he wandered back towards the house. Perfect! Score one for her inner stubborn teenager!

A couple of minutes later, she drew the tractor to a halt behind the broken-down van. She could see Basil sitting in a patch of sunlight, waiting for her. Killing the engine, she hopped down and ambled over towards him. Basil didn't budge other than to lift his head to give her optimal tickle access.

'Where's your dad, eh?' she whispered, looking over towards the van, and noticing that the bonnet was up.

Straightening up, Alice approached only to find Jake up to his elbows, rummaging deep in the bowels of the engine. There was something about the sight of him bent over wearing just a pair of shorts and a now seriously oily tee-shirt that did something funny to her insides. It really was quite a view!

'Don't think I'm going to have much luck with this,' said Jake, straightening up and running a filthy hand through his hair. 'At least, not without having a better look on some hard standing.'

'Right,' said Alice, hoping that her face wasn't as flushed as she felt. 'Well, that's okay – let's get you hitched up.'

'I'd better sort out somewhere for you to tow me to, first!' he laughed.

Alice shrugged. 'There's a decent bit of hard standing over by our boathouse. We'll take it there. At least it'll be safe and accessible and away from the road while you're getting it sorted out?'

Jake looked surprised but quickly smiled and nodded. 'Great – thanks!'

Alice hopped back up into the tractor and, setting it rumbling again, she lined herself up so that she could hitch the van up with the steel tow rope.

'It's not too far and the track is pretty straight,' she shouted down to Jake as he made sure everything was secure.

He promptly gave her a double thumbs-up.

Alice went to close the cab door when she noticed Basil attempting to hop up the steep couple of steps to join her.

'I think he wants to ride with you!' shouted Jake, amusement clear on his face. 'He loves tractors – but you should definitely be flattered – he usually takes forever to warm up to new people!'

Alice grinned and patted her thigh, inviting the grumpy dog into the cab with her. Jake shook his head and, bending over, scooped Basil up and deposited him into Alice's outstretched arms.

'He's a bit old – got arthritis!' yelled Jake over the rumbling of the engine.

Basil was incredibly heavy but given that he'd just

been unceremoniously handed over to a random stranger sitting in a tractor, he was being surprisingly well behaved.

Jake closed the cab door for her and then made his way back towards the van.

'Alright Basil,' said Alice, setting the wagging lump of dog down next to her seat and opening the window so that he could hang his head out into the fresh air, 'let's get this show on the road.'

They made a remarkably good team and in ten minutes the poor, broken van was parked up safely on the level piece of ground next to the old boathouse.

'Brilliant!' beamed Jake, nudging her gratefully with one elbow. 'That'll make it so much easier to work on... I might even be able to get underneath safely without running the risk of rolling down the bank into the river. Right, what now?'

'Time for your part of the bargain,' said Alice.

'And that would be...?' said Jake, grinning at her while managing to look wary at the same time.

'I'd love it if you could take a look at our visitors' centre.' Alice paused and let out a sigh. 'Well, what *would* have been our visitors' centre if the builders hadn't buggered off mid-job and left me in the lurch.'

'Oh dear,' said Jake, raising his eyebrows. 'Dare I ask?'

'I wouldn't,' muttered Alice darkly, before deciding that it would probably be best to lighten the mood – after all, they were mid mutual favour, and she didn't want to scare Jake off if there was *any* chance he might be willing to help them out. 'Hop up and I'll drive us back over to the house.'

One short tractor ride later where all three of them had squished like sardines into the tiny cab and they arrived back outside the barn. Jake and Basil hopped down before Alice tucked the old tractor safely away again.

'This way,' said Alice, leading her guests through the yard, past the various broken-down outbuildings and barns. 'Okay,' she said, resisting the urge to cross her fingers, 'have a good look around and see what you think! I just need to know how long it would take someone to sort it out and finish the work.'

'Okay – I can definitely do that!' said Jake.

She stepped back and let Jake go ahead of her, closely followed by Basil, excitedly wagging his tail at the chance of exploring this new territory. Alice followed the pair of them inside.

She soon discovered that looking around the quarter-finished space with someone new meant that she saw it in a very different light. It was in a state. Warren and his crew had just dropped tools and left before they were even half-done. She couldn't even bring herself to check out the side rooms – the main space was depressing enough.

Outside, parts of the roof still needed re-slating and the brickwork both inside and out needed pointing. A few of the windows desperately needed replacing and a lot of the woodwork was so rotten you could pull it away with your fingertips.

Alice had to bite her tongue to stop herself from treating Jake to a running commentary as he looked around. Eventually, he turned to her, gave a quick nod and gestured for her to follow him back out into the sunshine. He quietly looked the outside of the building over more carefully and then stared up at the roof.

Unable to restrain herself any longer, Alice turned to face him. 'So – is this the sort of work you've done before?' she asked. It was a straight question and she hoped that he'd give her a straight answer.

'Yes,' he said, simply.

Alice couldn't help but crack a smile at that. It was about as straight an answer as she could have hoped for. He hadn't even scratched his chin - something she couldn't help but like about him.

'I know it's a lot of work...' she said.

'It is, but it's all doable,' replied Jake.

Alice loved that confidence. It made the clouds of doom recede ever so slightly.

'It would probably take about a month to complete.'

Ah. Here came the clouds again.

'A month?' she breathed. She knew it wasn't really that long in the grand scheme of things, but it wouldn't get her out of this sticky spot when it came to finding somewhere to host *Knit One Pour One*.

'Yeah,' said Jake with a slight shrug. 'I mean, especially if it was just one person tackling most of it alone.'

Alice nodded. She knew she was being ridiculous even daring to dream it could be completed any sooner than that.

'Unfortunately, I've already asked quite literally everyone who might have been able to help. They're either not up for it or simply don't have the time.'

'What's the rush on it?' asked Jake, curiously.

Alice sighed. She knew she was going to look like a complete idiot, but there wasn't anything for it but to tell him about her plans for *Knit One Pour One*, opening the vineyard back up to the community and giving them a communal space to use.

'And the first one of these sessions is meant to take place-?'

'In just over a week,' said Alice on a long, resigned sigh.

Jake nodded and pottered to the end of the building, clearly checking out just how much work needed to be done to the walls. Alice followed him as he slowly skirted around the old stonework, taking it all in.

'The thing is, because the other builders were so sure when they'd be finished by, I set the date ages ago and invited everyone. There are posters everywhere and we even put a little advert in the local paper. Everyone seems so excited and they're going to be really disappointed if it doesn't happen.'

'Surely you could re-schedule though? Or maybe hold it in one of the other buildings?' said Jake, raising his eyebrows.

'If you think this one's a mess… well, let's just say that this is a five-star venue compared to the others!' Alice paused. 'Also, we've not had the best rep with the locals. Dad's quite… erm… private about the place, so they haven't exactly been welcomed here for a long time. This was meant to be the first step in encouraging them back to the vineyard… and now I'm going to have to let everyone down.'

Alice stopped talking – partly because of the large lump that had just formed in her throat and partly because Jake had come to a halt and was now staring at the scrubby piece of land that sat behind the visitors' centre.

'You know,' he said at last, turning from the epic patch of head-high brambles in front of them to grin at her, 'I might just have a plan that will work.'

'You do?' said Alice, unable to keep the surprise out of her voice.

Jake nodded. 'Yep – a way to get the visitors' centre finished, and give you somewhere to hold the first of your knitting thingies too.'

Alice swallowed, barely daring to say anything. Surely this was all far too good to be true?!

'What's the catch?' she said eventually.

'Well – as long as you don't mind me clearing this patch?' he said, pointing to the bramble jungle.

'Mind?' laughed Alice. 'Blimey, I'll even help!'

'Well, that's settled then,' said Jake with a nod.

Alice felt a tiny pinprick appear in her newfound optimism. 'Erm, what's settled?'

'I'll do the work for you and in return, me and Basil can hang out here while I get the van sorted.'

Alice considered this for a moment. It sounded perfect, apart from one thing. 'What about money?' she said awkwardly. 'The last builders-'

'Not really how I work,' said Jake, cutting her off with a smile.

'Erm… okay?' she said, confused.

'I usually work for free lodging, dog food, human food – and maybe a bit of help here and there with the van,' he said with a shrug.

'Sounds like a deal to me,' said Alice quickly. 'You could stay in the boathouse if you'd like? There'll be a bit more room in there for you than in the van.'

'Perfect!' said Jake.

'No. Sorry – it's really not!' laughed Alice. 'I absolutely love it in there, but it's in a bit of a state. But… if you don't mind a few spiders and no heating, it should be okay…' she trailed off, realising what she was offering him wasn't exactly brilliant.

'Seriously,' said Jake, giving her a soft smile, 'it sounds just the ticket. What do you reckon, Basil?' he asked.

Basil, who'd plonked his behind down on Jake's trainers, started to wag his tail, grinning up at them both.

'That settles it then,' laughed Jake. 'If Basil's happy, so am I.'

Alice stared at Jake's extended hand for a couple of seconds before reaching out and giving it a shake to seal the deal. He had a nice handshake, she decided. Firm and warm. She did her best to ignore the tingle of excitement that worked its way up her arm from the skin-on-skin contact.

For the second time this morning, she felt like a teenager again – and this time it felt amazing. This man was definitely having a very strange effect on her.

CHAPTER 4

*A*lice helped Jake to haul open the wooden double doors at the front of the boathouse and then led the way inside. She crossed her fingers in her pocket, hoping against hope that he wasn't going to change his mind about the whole thing when he saw what poor lodgings he was being offered.

The boathouse had remained untouched for years and had become a bit of a general dumping ground for unused bits and pieces that might come in useful at some point. It was full of random junk and housed various piles of unidentified, unremembered objects covered over with tarpaulins.

Alice made her way gingerly around a group of plastic buckets. They held a good collection of random rusty things that had probably been something incredibly useful once upon a time - before they'd corroded into an unrecognisable mass of orangey-brown.

'I'm sorry,' she said, shaking her head, 'I'd forgotten how bad it is in here – maybe this isn't such a great idea after all.'

'Are you kidding?' said Jake, peering around him. 'This is perfect... as long as you don't mind me tidying up a little bit, just to make a bit of space?'

'Of course!' said Alice, her smile returning as a swoop of relief ran through her. This all felt far too good to be true, but hey, who was she to knock it? If Jake thought the boathouse was perfect, she wasn't going to be the one to argue!

'May I?' said Jake, pointing at the huge tarp that was draped over the boat that took up most of the space at one side of the shed.

'Be my guest!' said Alice with a shrug. She watched as Jake lifted one corner of the tarp and peeked underneath.

'Nice!' said Jake with appreciation. 'Give me a hand?'

Alice nodded, grinning as she noticed that his eyes had lit up like a kid at Christmas. She moved forward and, grabbing the opposite corner of the tarp, helped him to drag it right back so that he could have a proper look at the boat.

'It hasn't been running for years,' she said, staring at the newly unearthed treasure in front of them. 'Apparently, there's something wrong with the engine.'

'Nothing a bit of TLC wouldn't sort, I bet,' Jake murmured, almost to himself.

Alice watched with a smile as Jake made his way around the side of the boat, giving it a tender pat here and there as he went.

'It used to be one of my dad's favourite pastimes – chugging around in that thing on the river. But we weren't able to get anyone to look at it… and then, well, it just sort of got forgotten. Just another thing on the endless list of jobs that need sorting out around here.'

Jake nodded. 'Well, she's a beauty,' he said. 'Erm - sorry to ask, but is your dad still around?'

Alice let out a surprised laugh. 'Oh yes, very much so. We live together in the main house. It's been just the two of us for years. He's a funny old sod, but I adore him. You'll meet him later…' She trailed off. Alice still wasn't quite sure how that was going to go yet, but she'd cross that bridge when she came to it.

First things first. She needed to make sure that Jake really was serious about staying.

'So, are you certain that this is okay for you? I mean – you don't mind camping out in here?'

'Absolutely. I love it,' said Jake with a smile. 'You know, I'm amazed a place like this hasn't been sold off and done up by some city type! It's just the sort of spot a Londoner would love to come down to a couple of times a year.'

Alice nodded. 'You're right. But we've got my dad to thank for making sure that hasn't happened. He's quite fierce when it comes to guarding this place. No matter how difficult things get, he would never divide the land up. Dad doesn't like change and he doesn't want this valley spoiled.'

'I really admire that,' said Jake.

'Me too – though there are bad bits about it too. He can be quite extreme. Quite precious about the vineyard. He took things a bit too far when it came to keeping people out - drove the local community away a bit.'

Jake nodded. 'Hence the signs down by the bridge?'

Alice nodded. 'I mean, you can see it from both sides, can't you? But we need our local community on side.'

'Nothing you can't fix – as long as you've got your dad on board?'

'Fingers crossed,' sighed Alice. 'He can be a stubborn old bugger. But I just want to create new links with our customers and our community. It's not like I want to sell anything off! My ex-boyfriend was always on at dad about the value of everything, and what he'd do with the vineyard if it belonged to him. I think it made dad even more nervy about it all if I'm honest. Warren would have developed every corner of the place and covered it in concrete by now.'

'He sounds like a real charmer,' muttered Jake, before quickly shaking his head. 'Sorry.'

Alice smiled at him. 'Don't be. And you're right. Let's just say my father wasn't too sorry when he became an ex.'

Jake nodded but didn't say anything, and suddenly Alice could kick herself for the fact that she'd just poured out an entire potted history of her family *and* relationship problems to this relative stranger. Poor bloke!

'Right, I'll leave you to settle in a bit?' she said quickly. 'There'll be food up at the house in the evenings – we eat at 6pm on the dot... sorry, that's a dad thing.'

'Great!' said Jake. 'Erm, one thing, I don't really have anything formal to wear!'

Alice smiled at him. 'Just come as you are. Or... well... maybe a clean tee-shirt would be a nice touch.'

Jake glanced down at his oil-spattered old tee-shirt and then grinned back at her. 'You've got it. And... would it be okay to bring Basil? It's just he doesn't like being on his own – especially in a strange place.'

'Of course,' she said. 'See you later then!'

As Alice ambled slowly back towards the farmhouse, she realised that she had rather a lot of explaining to do when she got there. How on earth was she going to tell her dad that a trespasser she'd found camping down by the bridge was now resident in their old boathouse? Add to that the fact that this random stranger had agreed to help with the visitors' centre and the situation quickly went from the sublime to the ridiculous!

Alice realised that, in her excitement, she'd forgotten to ask Jake about his idea to save the *Knit One*

Pour One event. Damn! She could really have done with that as extra ammo when she was talking to her dad.

Suddenly, the whole thing started to seem too good to be true. After all, she had absolutely no idea how competent he was when it came to the actual building work. In fact, she realised that she didn't know anything about him at all other than the fact that he had a broken-down van, owned a dog called Basil, had just been working on a remote Scottish island... and had a rather strange effect on her.

Crap! Still, even though she'd spent a lot of the morning feeling like a teenager, she was – in fact – a grown-up. She could fill her dad in without getting grounded. At least, she hoped she could!

Alice quietly let herself in through the backdoor and paused, listening for the tell-tale signs that would give her a clue where her dad was. Nothing – everything was completely quiet.

She tiptoed towards the kitchen and peered around the corner.

'Dad?' she said softly,

Nothing.

'Hellooo? Dad?' she called into the hallway.

Still nothing. Excellent. It didn't look like he was around after all. Her inner teenager gave a fist pump of triumph – she was going to get away with putting it off until later.

Alice mooched back into the kitchen, flicked the kettle on and flopped into one of the bentwood chairs with a weary sigh. What a morning! Still, at least something good had come out of what could have become a pretty awkward scenario.

She just hoped that Jake would actually be up to the job when he made a start on the work. Once she did finally get around to telling her dad about what was going on, perhaps it would be a good idea for the three of them to sit down and discuss the plan of action. Her dad would be able to see through any kind of nonsense if Jake *was* trying to string her along… but he really didn't seem the type, somehow.

At least she wasn't going to have to spend the afternoon ringing around to cancel *Knit One Pour One* – that really would have been soul-destroying.

Alice heaved herself back to her feet and began pulling out the ingredients to make a casserole for tea for the three of them. It could just sit on a low heat and do its thing for the afternoon. Everyone liked casserole… didn't they?

As she began slicing up some celery, her mind wandered to Lionel.

He was an incredible knitter, and even though it had sent her into a bit of a tail-spin earlier, she was glad that he was planning on making the trip to join them. She wished that she'd tried harder when he'd attempted to teach her to knit as a little girl. That hadn't gone so well and she'd ended up all tangled up and had to be cut out of a massive nest of wool. The memory made her smile.

Considering that she'd never actually managed to learn to knit, the fact that she was kicking things off at the vineyard with a knitting group might seem odd to some people. The thing was, there had been such a sense of excitement about the idea when she'd first mentioned it to a few people in the village that it had taken on a bit of a life of its own. There was a definite sense that it was something the locals wanted to do.

Alice reckoned the fact that there would be a good selection of the vineyard's wine available to taste had quite a lot to do with everyone's levels of enthusiasm. She had to admit that she was yet to be convinced – somehow, mixing wine and wool sounded like a recipe for disaster. Still, she was looking forward to seeing how the experiment turned out!

Hopefully, it would give their wine sales a bit of a boost locally if people tried it, loved it and recommended it to their friends. Still, at least with Lionel coming to *Knit One Pour One*, there would be one guaranteed wine sale for the evening.

As she reached for some potatoes to add to the mix, Alice's mind wandered back towards the boathouse. She wondered how her dad was going to react to a complete stranger moving in. Arthur Merryfield *wasn't* good with strangers. He wasn't particularly good with people full stop. Perhaps it would have been better if she'd run the whole thing past him before agreeing to anything with Jake... But hey, it was done. Her dad would just have to deal with it!

Alice bit her lip. It might be a bit awkward at first... but there had been quite a few awkward moments with her father recently. The real whopper had been when she'd given Warren the visitors' centre work in the first place. In that case, her dad had been right to worry.

Having her ex-boyfriend working here had been a mistake on so many different levels – she could see that now. For starters, his crew hadn't exactly exhibited much urgency in getting on with the work at hand. Most of the time they hadn't shown up until after ten in the morning. Then they'd take long lunch breaks in the pub over at Little Bamton – and most of the time, they never bothered to return for the afternoon. Some days they'd worked less than two hours.

Alice let out a little growl and chucked a handful of chopped spuds into a large silver saucepan with a little more force than was strictly necessary. She couldn't help but kick herself every time she thought about Warren. How could she have believed for a second that the guy had changed? He was still a selfish, self-obsessed twit. To think she'd been on the verge of giving him a second chance!

CHAPTER 5

*A*lice glanced at the old clock on the kitchen wall. It was already ten past six and neither her father nor Jake had appeared for their tea. Of course, she didn't know Jake well enough – or at all, in fact – to be able to tell if this was normal for him. Some people seemed to manage to be late for everything. But she *did* know her father.

Arthur Merryfield was a stickler for punctuality – especially when it came to mealtimes. He'd always made sure that the pair of them sat down together for a meal every evening at exactly six o'clock. It was a rule that was never relaxed – even on the rare occasions they had guests to stay.

Alice sighed. At least the casserole wouldn't spoil. She'd give it five more minutes and then she'd have to go in search of them – starting with her dad. She'd been waiting to have a word with him all afternoon.

She still needed to tell him about Jake and the rather unconventional deal she'd managed to agree with him. Unusually - and typically - her dad had been awol all afternoon.

Right. It was no good. She was going to have to go and hunt for him. It would be a total disaster if the pair of them managed to run into each other without her there to mediate. She slid the saucepan to the cooler end of the stove, grabbed her cardigan from the back of her chair and made her way outside.

The sweet, soft air washed over her the minute she stepped through the backdoor, and Alice paused to take a long breath. Birdsong was drifting on the breeze and she closed her eyes, trying to differentiate between the different calls. Blackbird, wren, wood pigeon, robin. This really was a very special place to live – if only she could remember to stop and appreciate it a bit more often.

Opening her eyes, Alice tried to decide where to start looking for her father. Maybe the winery would be the best place to start in case he'd become engrossed in a job and lost track of time.

She made her way towards the large building and let herself into the cool, cavernous space. It was still and quiet in here. Her eyes raked the spaces between the stainless-steel vats, but it was obvious by the silence that her dad wasn't in here working.

A little spike of worry went through her. What if

something had happened to him? He could be lying hurt somewhere and she wouldn't have a clue.

Alice had been about to leave the building, but she turned back and did a more thorough sweep of the long, barrel-lined aisles. No, he really wasn't in here.

Next, she checked the barn where the tractor stood, followed by his workshop and all the other various outbuildings. There was absolutely no sign of her dad anywhere. Of course, he could be out working on the vines somewhere, but that had never stopped him from turning up on time for his tea before!

Alice made her way back out into the fresh air, wracking her brains and trying to decide where she should search next. It was becoming more and more difficult to ignore the worry that was mounting in her chest.

The sharp sounds of a dog barking cut through her anxious thoughts. Basil! At least he would lead her to Jake. Maybe he'd help her look for her dad.

Basil's continued barking led Alice down towards the river, and she took the path at a bit of a trot. When she reached the bank that overlooked the deep, gentle bend beyond the boathouse, she stopped dead, staring.

Alice blinked a couple of times to check that she hadn't randomly started to hallucinate. No - it was real, alright! The boat she'd helped Jake to uncover earlier was now motoring around in the centre of the wide river. She'd been absolutely certain that the old boat had needed repair - but that wasn't what had her gaping in surprise.

In the back of the boat sat Jake, her dad, and Basil – barking his head off in pure delight. What on earth was her dad doing with Jake? Oh crap, he'd have her guts for garters now!

Or… maybe not.

Jake turned his head and, spotting her watching them from the bank, raised his hand in a wave. Her dad followed suit, waving merrily with one hand as the other rested on Basil's head. Jake turned the boat around and the three of them headed back in her direction.

Judging by the three matching grins, the trio had been having a whale of a time. Basil moved to sit in the bow, looking like royalty as he yapped a greeting to her.

Once Jake had secured the boat, the three of them waded ashore, unable to wipe the wide smiles from their faces.

'You're late for dinner,' she said, crossing her arms and faking a frown. She wasn't cross. Not even slightly. Maybe a little bit confused – but how could she be angry when her dad was looking the happiest she'd seen him in decades?

'I'm so sorry, Alice!' said Jake. 'We lost track of time…'

'How… what…?' Alice wasn't quite sure how to begin, so she just pointed at the boat and quirked an eyebrow at her father, who grinned back at her sheepishly.

'Well,' he said, 'I bumped into Jake earlier when I spotted this random van sitting by the boathouse – and we got talking about the boat and the engine... and we managed to fix it!'

Alice watched in amusement as her father looked to Jake for backup as if they were two naughty schoolboys.

Jake promptly nodded, his eyes wide and innocent. 'Yeah – and then, well, we thought we'd better test it out in the water.'

'Right,' said Alice, biting back a laugh as she looked the pair of them over. They were wet through and covered in mud. It was clear that her father had loved every second of it.

A wave of relief washed over her. It looked very much like she was off the hook when it came to explaining to her dad about Jake staying in the boathouse for a while.

'So – you don't mind that Jake's going to be staying while he gets the van sorted out?' she asked lightly, deciding to capitalise on her dad's good mood while she could.

'Mind? Anyone that good with engines is okay in my book,' chuckled Arthur, bumping his elbow into Jake's.

'Cheers, Arthur,' laughed Jake, bending to give Basil a scratch behind the ears.

'We've already got plans to mend some of the other stuff that's just littering the place up!' said Arthur, rubbing his hands together in excitement. 'Jake's more than welcome to stay for as long as he likes. And Basil – he makes an excellent cabin boy.'

Alice rolled her eyes. 'Well, that's great. But right now, there's a casserole with your names on it.'

'Excellent!' said Arthur.

'You know, I was worried when you two didn't turn up for dinner!'

She watched the identical grins disappear as both the naughty children in front of her began to apologise, hanging their heads in front of the only adult in the vicinity.

Alice started to laugh. 'It's fine – no harm done. Come on, let's head up to the house and have something to eat!'

The four of them made their way back up the path, and as soon as they reached the house Alice dispatched the two men for a much-needed wash.

There were several bathrooms in the large farmhouse, most of which were barely ever used, but in rare cases like this they came in handy. Arthur sloped off to take a shower while Alice led Jake up to a guest bathroom on the first floor. She grabbed a huge, slightly knackered bath sheet from the airing cupboard on the way past.

'Right,' she said, pushing open the door and breaking the strange silence that had grown between them, 'the taps are a bit temperamental. You have to kind of twist and hold? There's a bit of a knack to getting the hot water out.'

Jake watched her closely as she demonstrated and then proceeded to get it right the first time.

'Impressive!' she laughed. 'That usually takes quite a bit of practice.'

Jake shrugged. 'Trust me, I've stayed in a few houses on the islands where the plumbing was even worse!'

Alice smiled and then realising she was still hugging the bath sheet to her chest, quickly handed it over.

'Great, thanks,' said Jake, taking it and then bending to swish his hand in the bath, testing the temperature.

Alice watched his fingers trail through the water as if mesmerised. He'd be taking his clothes off again, just like down at the river. Taking his clothes off in *her* house.

'So…' said Jake, tilting his head in amusement and glancing at the door.

Oops! She'd completely forgotten about the part where she needed to leave the room so that he could actually get undressed.

'Right,' she said, shaking herself out of it. 'I'll, um, I'll leave you to it.'

She quickly made her way out of the bathroom, closing the door behind her. The doorknob promptly fell off in her hand. Bloody typical.

'Jake?' she called.

'Yeah?'

'The doorknob just came off in my hand!

'Don't worry, I'll sort it.'

Alice could swear she could hear laughter in his voice.

'Well, okay,' she said, 'I'll leave you to it, but I'll come back with a rescue party in twenty minutes if you haven't managed to let yourself out by then!'

Back in the kitchen, Alice discovered that Basil had already curled up in front of the stove. She smiled down at him. He fitted, somehow - the little dog already felt like a part of the family – but that was ridiculous, wasn't it? She'd only met him that morning!

'Ah, that's better!'

Alice turned to find her dad standing behind her, fresh from the shower, his newfound smile still fixed firmly on his face.

'You comfy there, boy?' he said, noticing Basil's new spot.

Alice watched her dad, reeling slightly from the change that had come over him. She hadn't seen this side of him for ages. Actually, she wasn't sure she'd *ever* seen this side of him. What on earth was going on? Some strange kind of magic seemed to be at work.

She quickly busied herself, cutting thick slices of fresh bread to go with the casserole as her dad made himself comfortable in his usual spot at the table behind her.

'Jake's going to take a look at the Massey Ferguson while he's here,' said Arthur. 'And that old pump I've been wanting to look at. And a bunch of other things. Brilliant, eh?'

'Definitely,' said Alice weakly, still trying to get her head around it all.

'He said he's not likely to stay for too long because he likes to keep moving – so we'd better start making a list of things for him to take a look at while he's here!'

Alice turned and placed the plate of bread in the centre of the table before straightening up and facing her dad properly.

'Don't forget the main reason he's here is to get the visitors' centre finished. That was the deal.'

Her dad simply grinned and shrugged at her. 'I'm sure there'll be plenty of time for some of the other stuff too. What a stroke of luck he broke down at the bridge!'

Alice raised her eyebrows but bit her lip to stop her from saying something she might regret. Still, she couldn't help but wonder whether his reaction might have been a bit different if the person that had broken down on their land hadn't been *quite* so good at fixing things. Somehow, she had a feeling that would have been a totally different story.

'Erm, hi!'

Jake's voice made Alice whirl around. He was standing in the doorway, holding up what looked to be a broken toothbrush.

'I'm really sorry – I had to use this to get the door open, and it snapped. I'll replace it! Or maybe I can take a look at your plumbing while I'm here to make up for it?'

Alice let out a snort of laughter, and Arthur started chuckling in his chair.

'Don't you worry about that, lad. That toothbrush must be at least twenty years old.'

Jake grinned as Alice put her foot on the pedal bin to open it up for him to toss the snapped handle inside.

'Yeah,' she said, wrinkling her nose, 'you know, I'm not even sure who it used to belong to!'

CHAPTER 6

*A*lice stretched and peeped at her bedside clock before wriggling further down under her cosy duvet. She was awake a bit later than usual, but she wasn't in any kind of rush to leave the comfort of her bed just yet. Just this once, she wanted to snuggle down and revel in the fact that things felt… good.

The previous evening had been terrific fun. The three of them had eaten their fill and the conversation hadn't stopped flowing – especially when her dad unearthed a couple of bottles of the vineyard's finest to sample. Jake had soon switched back to cups of tea, but she hadn't. She'd been having too much fun.

It was just so nice to have some company in the house that her father didn't despise – and Jake was certainly brilliant company. He'd journeyed all over the place and was more than happy to share stories from his travels.

Alice grinned to herself under the safety of her duvet. She'd definitely had a bit too much to drink, but she was fairly certain that she hadn't embarrassed herself... which was a miracle considering that she'd found it increasingly difficult to keep her eyes off of their guest's lively face. He was just so... alive? Maybe *present* was a better word for it?

Whatever it was, he was as generous with his conversation as he seemed to be with his actions, and she'd watched the easy friendship that he'd already struck up with her father with delight.

Everything had definitely become a bit foggy by the end of the evening and Alice could feel the rumble of a headache lurking in the background this morning.

After Jake had helped her to clear away the dinner things last night, they'd got the plans for the visitors' centre out and spread them across the kitchen table. Jake had asked some interesting questions about how they wanted things done, and it had been impossible not to compare his open and curious manner with the way Warren dealt with things. Her ex thought he knew everything and therefore didn't bother to listen to anyone else.

Alice popped her head out from under the covers again and hastily clambered out of bed. She didn't really want to be thinking about Warren in the cosy glow of a new day. She wandered over to the window and peeped out through the gap in the curtains. It was sunny again.

Turning back to her room, she eyeballed her trainers that were sitting just underneath her chest of drawers where she'd kicked them off the day before. Should she go for a run? It was gorgeous out there and it would probably do her hangover good. But… maybe not today. She didn't feel like it. She turned back to the window and then frowned.

Actually - definitely not today. Something was going on down by the visitors' centre. She could hear muffled bangs and crashes drifting up to her and she wondered what on earth was going on. She needed to get dressed and go and investigate.

Alice hastily threw some clothes on and hot-footed it downstairs and out through the back door. Making her way around the back of the visitors' centre, she gaped at the sight that met her eyes. Sitting on the scruffy patch of ground just outside the door were several sheets of plasterboard, a pile of ugly PVC, double-glazed window units and a massive roll of lino. Alice pulled a face. It was a strange, lurid green and had a pattern of fake flagstones pressed into its surface.

Next to these was a large pile of what looked like strip-light fittings – at least, Alice guessed that's what they were. What on earth was going on? None of this had been here yesterday…

'Morning!' said Jake, grinning at her as he appeared from the depths of the building carrying an armful of silicone sealant tubes, Basil trotting at his heels.

'Erm… hi!' said Alice, staring at him as he tipped the

tubes onto the grass next to the light fittings before patting Basil's head. 'What's all this lot?'

Jake raised his eyebrows. 'It's all the stuff your builders left behind in there. It was piled up in that little side room you want to turn into a toilet. I just thought it'd be better to tidy it up and get it out the way for a moment so that I can make a start. Hope that's okay?'

Jake watched her uncertainly as Alice shook her head. She couldn't believe this!

'This was all in there?' she said, her voice faint.

'Yes,' said Jake, clearly confused. 'Like I said, it was tucked away in the bit that you're turning into a loo.'

'But... I didn't agree to them buying anything like this,' she said, pointing at the roll of hideous green lino. 'I mean, the work was supposed to complement the old building. I *told* them I didn't want to spoil it with stuff like this. That's why dad and I gave them such a big budget for materials - so that we could have proper flagstones and wooden windows.'

She took a deep breath, realising that her voice had become so shrill that she'd be calling in the dolphins if she wasn't careful. 'Besides,' she added, relieved that it came out in a slightly more human tone, 'the planning states that the windows *have* to be wooden. Certainly not these monstrosities. I wonder how much they spent...'

'Actually, they left a pile of receipts on the windowsill in there,' said Jake. 'I'll grab them...'

Two seconds later, Jake returned with a wad of receipts and handed them over to her. Alice flicked through them, her heart hammering.

Well – *bang* went her nice, peaceful sense of calm! It didn't take a great deal of mental arithmetic to figure out that Warren had managed to waste a great deal of the materials budget on a bunch of stuff that was completely inappropriate for the job.

Clearly, the idiot had been up to his old tricks. He'd obviously ignored all the guidelines he'd been given - including those set by their lovely planning officer - and had decided to do the work using a bunch of cheap, modern building materials instead. Well – not *that* cheap, as it turned out.

'Shit,' she breathed.

'My thoughts entirely,' said Jake, giving the pile of plasterboard a filthy look. 'Actually, while you're here, I've got a couple of quick questions... if you don't mind?'

Alice nodded and followed Jake inside in a daze, leaving Basil to stretch out in a patch of sun on the grass.

Jake led her through the main space and into the smaller room beyond that was destined to become to the toilet where he'd discovered all the building materials. They hadn't bothered looking in here when she'd been showing him around - why would she, when there was so much work to do in the rest of the place? Even so...

Jake pointed but he didn't really need to say anything. Half the old, beautiful brickwork that had been due to be restored had already been hidden behind sheets of plasterboard.

'*Not* the plan,' she muttered, feeling a swell of anger flare up inside her. She wasn't sure if it was at Warren for so blatantly ignoring what he'd been asked to do, or at herself for not knowing this had been going on. She should have kept a closer eye on things. No – she should have just avoided giving him the work in the first place!

'Do you mind if I remove it?' asked Jake.

Alice shook her head. 'Not at all – if you think we can without damaging anything?'

Jake nodded. 'At least it's just in here and not the main space... anyway, it looks like they've just put a flimsy bit of framing up. It hasn't really been anchored like it should have.'

Ten minutes later, Alice was wearing a pair of safety goggles from Jake's toolbox as she helped him to remove the plasterboard from the wall, chunk by chunk.

As she shifted another damaged, half-sheet out of the building and added it to the pile outside, she couldn't help the small smile that crept onto her face. She had to hand it to Jake – when he decided to do something, it certainly didn't take him very long to make a start!

'You know,' said Jake, as she made her way back to where he was now attacking the flimsy wooden framing as if it had personally insulted him, 'I reckon you've had a lucky escape.'

'What do you mean?' Alice muttered, tensing up. She didn't much feel like discussing her failed relationship with Warren. Not right now, while she was feeling like such a plonker for thinking it had been a good idea to invite him back into her life in any way, shape or form.

'The fact that your builders buggered off before getting any further with the job,' said Jake, pausing to wipe the back of his hand across his dusty forehead. 'A couple more days of Warren's *building,* and he'd have ruined this place forever. Thank goodness they were slow workers!'

Alice nodded. She had to agree – though she was still reeling from the fact that he'd had the nerve to completely ignore everything they'd talked about. But then – why should it be such a surprise? This kind of thing was Warren's signature move. Lazy, half-arsed, and thinking he knew better. It had his name all over it, didn't it?

'I'm so glad they didn't get the chance to tear out the old wooden windows yet,' he said, heading over and running his hand lovingly along the rotten and pitted sill.

'They're in such a state,' sighed Alice, her mind flying to the PVC monstrosities that lay waiting for them outside. 'I'd budgeted for new, wooden frames – and he's gone for those plastic things that we can't even use even if we wanted to. And...'

Alice took a deep breath. She had to be straight with Jake, didn't she? He *had* to know the truth of it.

'Look,' she said, 'we're living hand to mouth a bit here at the moment. We saved up every bit of spare cash we had for all the materials for this place – and now... well, Warren's blown most of it on that pile of rubbish outside.'

Jake nodded, his brow creasing in a frown.

'We're not going to be able to get the wooden frames... and my planning guy would have a fit if we used the PVC ones!'

'Maybe we can figure this out,' said Jake in a quiet voice, inspecting the window more closely. 'I mean, sure, these are in a pretty bad way, but I reckon I can bring them back to life with a bit of timber and the right tools.'

'Really?' said Alice, her heart lifting a little, but not daring to believe it was possible.

'Sure,' said Jake, 'I found some stuff in the boathouse when I was tidying up yesterday that might be just the thing.'

'You did?'

This was officially sounding too good to be true, and Alice promptly reminded herself that no matter how confident Jake sounded, they hadn't actually seen him in action yet. Unless you counted getting her dad's boat fixed and back in the water on his first day here. But that was an engine, not a building. Not the fiddly restoration of knackered, wooden windowsills!

'Shall we go and check it out?' said Jake.

Alice stared at him for a beat and then shrugged.

'Sure!' she said, because why not? What did she really stand to lose at this point? The money was spent and all she had to show for it was that ghastly heap outside the door.

'You know,' said Jake, as they strode together down the stony path that led towards the boathouse with Basil trotting along between them, 'I unearthed all sorts of treasures when I started moving those tarpaulins around yesterday.'

'I'm not surprised,' said Alice, shooting him a weary smile.

Unlike a lot of the outbuildings that surrounded the old farmhouse, the boathouse was at least watertight. This meant that it had become a useful dumping ground for all sorts of bits and pieces that weren't needed anymore but "might come in handy one day," as her dad was fond of saying.

'Seriously,' said Jake, 'there are probably quite a few things in there that we can salvage and use for the project – as long as you and your dad don't mind.'

'Mind?' laughed Alice. 'I can pretty much guarantee

you that if it's in there, it's been completely forgotten about and is up for grabs.'

As they approached the boathouse with the van sitting outside, Alice stood back to let Jake open the doors. Yesterday it had been different – she'd been the host. But now? Well, now this was Jake's home... however grotty and temporary.

Jake quickly pulled the doors open wide and then led the way inside, with Alice and Basil bringing up the rear. Alice promptly ground to a halt, staring around her in surprise.

The boathouse had been transformed. Jake must have been up half the night tidying it up. In fact, the word "tidying" didn't even cover it! The deep shelves along the back wall had clearly been emptied, cleaned down and re-stacked with care. Everything was arranged meticulously rather than just being shoved in wherever it would fit, with the layers showing the strata of junk from across the decades.

Now that the old boat was back on the river where it belonged, there was loads more floor space too. Jake had made himself a cosy-looking bedding area near the shelves and had even arranged a few books on one of the lower ledges next to a battery-powered lantern. To finish off his "bedroom" he'd commandeered an old wicker chair she vaguely recognised from childhood and covered it with a bright blanket. Basil promptly hopped up onto it, turned in a circle and settled down for a nap.

'I unearthed this lot,' said Jake, pointing to a whole heap of dusty wooden chairs at the other side of the shed. 'I thought they might be good for your knitting club!'

Alice stared at them. She remembered these too. They'd always been pulled out whenever they'd had parties at the house when she was really little - back when her mum had been alive. They were gorgeous old things, but now they were filthy and creaky, and several looked like they needed repairing.

'They would be great… but…'

'Nothing a bit of hot, soapy water followed by half an hour drying in the sun and a fresh lick of paint wouldn't cure!' said Jake cheerily. 'Beautiful old things – they deserve a fresh lease of life.'

Alice smiled at him. There was something about Jake that was so… unusual. The way he was talking about this dusty old pile of wooden furniture as if it was something special - something to be cherished.

Seeing the chairs again took her right back to when she was a child, surrounded by happy chatter at one of her parents' parties. Back when her mum had still been around - before her dad had closed their doors on the rest of the world.

'Oh,' said Jake, excitedly hopping over towards a couple of boxes on an old side table, completely oblivious to the wave of emotion that had just crashed over her, 'I left these out for you to look at!'

Alice wandered over, glad to have an excuse not to

have to say anything for a moment as she opened the boxes for a look. One was full of long strings of hand-made bunting. The other held strands of multi-coloured lights. The boxes clearly hadn't been opened in years.

'Amazing the mice didn't get at them!' said Jake. 'I unravelled the whole lot to check them over – and they're completely fine! Aren't they gorgeous?!'

Alice nodded, blinking hard as more memories of long, lazy summer evenings surfaced – the lights and bunting swaying in the breeze as tinkling laughter drifted across the vineyard.

'You okay?' said Jake.

Alice forced a smile and nodded. 'These will be perfect for decorating the visitors' centre when it's finally finished.'

Jake nodded enthusiastically.

Alice watched him for a moment as he began rummaging in another box, and then stared around her. The boathouse had been completely transformed in just one night... all because someone had shown it a little bit of love. It was wonderful, and somehow scary at the same time, what a difference a little bit of love could make.

CHAPTER 7

*A*fter earmarking some timber that Jake had found stacked under a tarpaulin for renovating the windows in the visitors' centre, they made their way back outside, leaving Basil snoozing in the chair.

Alice watched as Jake flung open the back doors of his van and hauled out a trug of hand tools. He still hadn't told her what his cunning plan for holding *Knit One Pour One* was and she decided that she couldn't wait any longer.

'Erm, Jake…' she started, tentatively, 'yesterday, you said you had an idea that might solve my problem with my knitting group's first meeting…'

'I was just getting to that bit!' laughed Jake, hauling a couple more boxes and bags out of the van and carefully placing them against the side before hopping up and disappearing into the back. 'Actually,' he said, popping his head back around the corner, 'I could use your help with something.'

'Sure!' said Alice in surprise, striding forward.

'Here,' he said. Bending low, he started to shove something extremely bulky towards her with a great deal of grunting.

As it came closer, Alice found herself looking at a vast, flattened roll of multi-coloured canvas.

'If you can grab it from your end?' said Jake, as he struggled to slide it any further.

Alice nodded and, reaching forward, got a grip on the massive chunk of fabric and started to pull. It was ridiculously heavy, huge and incredibly dusty. As she helped to manhandle it over the edge and towards the gravel, it proved to be as much as they could do to bundle it out of the back of the van between them.

'That's a tent!' puffed Alice once they'd let it flop down onto the ground.

'Bingo!' said Jake with a grin, jumping down and gathering together the guy ropes that had trailed behind it. 'A great big circus tent that I picked up in Ireland in return for doing a bit of stone walling for someone. It's in pretty good condition... just as long as it doesn't rain. I mean, you might have to have a few buckets on standby!'

'For *Knit One Pour One*, you mean?' asked Alice in delight, bending low and stroking the bright, striped canvas.

'Yep!' said Jake with a grin. 'I mean, it needs

unrolling and airing – I've been using it as a mattress for the last two years! What do you think?'

'I think it's brilliant!' she beamed at him. 'Can we have a proper look?'

'Why not!' said Jake. 'If you're up for giving me a hand again – we'll drag it into the boathouse and unroll it in there. Then at least if the weather turns, we won't have to worry about shifting it in a hurry.'

Between them, with rather a lot of grunting and groaning and a tiny bit of swearing, they managed to drag it into the boathouse. After shifting a few things out of the way, Alice gave Jake a hand to unroll it.

She gasped as they opened it up. It was a beautiful old thing. It was mainly made of heavy red and cream striped canvas, but a patchwork of other materials had been added over the years - clearly used to mend various holes and tears here and there.

'It's going to look so cute when it's full of knitters!' said Alice with a grin.

Jake nodded. 'I just need to sort out a tent pole or two – but I spotted several old masts hidden away at the back there then I was tidying up.' He pointed to the far corner where several wooden and fibreglass poles were resting up against the wall.

'They're from the old dinghies,' said Alice. 'No problem using them if you think they'll be useful!'

Jake nodded. 'I reckon they'll do the trick nicely. And there's a large heap of rope over there too – so we're covered if we find any of the guy ropes need changing.'

'Perfect!' said Alice, bouncing on her toes as excitement started to fizz in her stomach.

'So - the question is - are you sure the knitters won't mind having their first meeting in a circus tent?'

Alice shook her head, feeling like the weight of the world had fallen from her shoulders. 'No. I think it'll be quite the opposite, actually – I think they'll love it. I mean – it's going to be magical when we've put it up and I've had the chance to decorate the inside a bit – especially compared to the old village hall.'

'I didn't know there was one!' said Jake, turning to her with interest.

'There isn't anymore,' said Alice, 'It's been empty for years - completely derelict now and no one has the cash to do it up.'

She stared down again at the colourful folds of the tent on the ground in front of her and gave a little wriggle of delight.

What a relief – this was just brilliant! How one earth could she ever thank Jake enough for saving her skin like this?

She turned towards him, wanting to at least *try* to explain what his help meant to her, when her foot caught in the edge of the canvas and she toppled.

Jake's arms went around her in seconds, catching her before she crashed down onto the hard floor.

'Gotcha!' he laughed, cradling her to him.

Alice's heart was racing. The happy, fizzing bubbles in her chest seemed to have doubled their efforts, and she felt breathless as she stared up into Jake's gorgeous eyes. Eyes that never seemed to stop smiling.

Before she knew what she was doing, before she could even think about it, Alice leaned forward and kissed him. She felt Jake freeze for a split second. Maybe she should pull back - tell him it was an accident. But then he drew her closer, and she melted into him. Nope - this *definitely* wasn't an accident. It felt too amazing to be an accident.

'Sorry,' she breathed when Jake eventually set her back on her feet. She blinked, feeling dazed.

Shit. How awkward?

Jake was smiling at her, and there was a definite twinkle in his eye as he shrugged amiably. He clearly didn't mind that she'd just practically jumped on him.

But Alice suddenly realised that she *did* mind. She really shouldn't have done that. What on earth was she thinking? She didn't want to ruin everything by falling for this amazing guy who'd appeared out of nowhere… this strange man with his adorable dog and clapped-out old van and the unsettling power to turn everything he touched into some kind of magic.

'Sorry,' she said again, her voice low and uncertain. 'I'd better go!'

Without saying another word, Alice beat a hasty retreat out of the boathouse, leaving both Jake and Basil staring after her in surprise.

. . .

Alice decided that the best course of action would be to pretend that the kiss hadn't happened. She'd close it up in a tiny box in her mind, shove it on a high shelf, and head into the village to stop her from obsessing. After all, she had a few things to sort out now that *Knit One Pour One* was definitely back on the agenda. For a start, she needed to organise some kind of food for the evening.

It was quite a long walk down into the village, but right now, Alice didn't mind that one bit. She needed to clear her head. Jake seemed to be having a bewildering effect on her. She'd never normally behave like that – throwing herself at a relative stranger. Nope... she wasn't going to think about that right now!

Alice crossed the bridge off of their land and then followed the pathway along the hedgerow in the direction of the village. It was thick with fragrant, creamy hawthorn blossom and the scent wound around her, calming her nerves.

Alice might have a few lingering regrets in the back of her mind about not spreading her wings when she was younger – but there was no doubt in her heart that this valley would always be home. She truly loved it. So what if she didn't have anything much to compare it to? Anything that made her heart sing like this had to be something special, didn't it?

Of course, there wasn't *any* other reason her heart

might be singing this morning, was there? Thundering in her chest and almost tripping her up with its excitable beat. Nope. Not at all. Nothing to do with soft lips and crinkling, smiling eyes... anyway, she wasn't meant to be thinking about that, was she?

Alice passed the sign to the village and promptly yanked her thoughts back to the matter at hand. The question was... who should she ask to help her out with food for *Knit One Pour One*?

There was Marjorie who made bonkers cakes from things she liked to forage from the hedgerows. They usually tasted delicious but sometimes there were bits of twig in them that would get caught in your teeth. Plus, the icing could be a bit hit and miss too. All very good for you, she was certain, but she wasn't sure her guests would appreciate the extra roughage! Besides, maybe cake, knitting needles and wool wouldn't be the best mix.

There was always Gloria, of course, but her house was right down by the river on the other side of the village. Her sandwiches were legendary. The thing was, Alice wasn't entirely sure how many people were going to turn up. Then there would be the issue of making sure that the fillings would suit everyone's dietary requirements.

She sighed. It could all be a bit of a waste of time if no one showed up. Which could happen. In fact, she'd seen it happen before – everyone getting behind an idea and then the enthusiasm waning when the day itself came around. An empty tent with a pile of sand-wiches would be decidedly dispiriting.

Goodness, she hoped that didn't happen. She'd spent so long badgering her father about welcoming the village back into their lives – it would be awful if no one came. The last thing she wanted to do was rein-force her father's hermit-like tendencies if this project of hers backfired.

Right. Decision made. Not sandwiches. That left her with one person she could call on for help. She'd go and visit Nell. She just hoped that her geese were in a good mood this morning!

CHAPTER 8

*F*red and Hazel stared intently at her through the wooden fence, and Alice glared back at them, trying to gauge the situation.

It was always a bit hit and miss visiting Nell's house. Getting past the geese was a dangerous sport, and you never quite knew what was going on behind their beady eyes. This morning, the perilous pair were busy chattering away to each other. To a stranger, they would probably look friendly enough – almost like some idyllic scene from a children's story.

But Alice knew better. She'd been chased around this front garden enough times to know that appearances could be deceiving. In fact, this pair of feathery terrors had the most volatile tempers in the whole valley. There was nothing worse than sprinting around with these two bringing up the rear, hissing their heads off with their necks outstretched as they tried to get a grip on the backs of your ankles.

She moved cautiously towards the gate, but for a change, the birds didn't follow her. They seemed to have turned their attention back to the grass as they gently grazed away at it, still chattering to each other in a friendly fashion. Right, she'd risk it. She carefully opened the little wooden gate, sidled through the gap and closed it quickly behind her with a gentle bump. That's all it took for the terrible two to turn their attention back to her.

Intent on investigating the newcomer, they waddled quickly towards her. Alice raised her hands up out of the way, valuing her fingers too much to leave them at pecking level and then stood stock-still. She watched them, trying to gauge what their next move might be while she was still within vaulting distance of the gate.

After pottering around her in a circle, peering at her intently while Alice held her breath, they suddenly decided to let her off the hook for the day. Alice couldn't tell if it was because they recognised her, or that they simply couldn't be bothered with terrorising her ankles because the sun was out. Either way, she breathed a sigh of relief as they bumbled off to investigate the slug content of one of the flower borders.

Phew! At least she wasn't going to have to sprint laps of Nell's front garden - she wasn't sure the vestiges of her hangover would have been up for a game of catch this morning!

Alice turned towards the cottage door and broke into a grin. She'd just spotted the real reason for the birds' retreat – Nell was standing there waiting for her.

'I was wondering if I might get a visit!' she said, beaming at Alice. 'Come on in before Fred and Hazel decide you're fair game again!'

Alice followed Nell, gladly closing the door on the geese before making her way through to the kitchen. She'd always loved this cottage. It was a gorgeous old place – much like the farmhouse at the vineyard, in that it was unchanged and all the better for it.

Where it differed, however, was that it was perhaps a little bit cleaner and tidier around the edges. Alice had to admit that she and her father existed in a state of barely-managed chaos. Sure, the hoover did get flung around when one of them remembered to do it, but things did have a habit of creeping up on them a bit.

Nell's cottage, on the other hand, was a haven of cosy, orderly calm. On top of that, it was beautifully familiar. Alice had been coming here for as long as she could remember, and as she sank into her usual spot at the kitchen table, she felt some of the weirdness of the morning leave her.

'Tea?' asked Nell, not bothering to wait for an answer before filling the kettle at the old butler's sink and popping it on the gas stove.

'Please!' said Alice. 'Anyway, what's the news? Why were you expecting a visit?'

Nell turned to her with a frown. 'Well, just that Warren's been busy telling everyone your knitting club's off.'

'*What?!*' gasped Alice.

'It's not then?' said Nell.

'No. Definitely not,' she spluttered.

'He said you'd scrapped the idea,' said Nell.

Alice bit back a few choice swear words. This was *not* the place to let them slip out. She'd never, *ever*, sworn in front of Nell, and she wasn't about to start now just because Warren was being a f-

'He's an idiot,' Alice growled.

'Well, yes,' laughed Nell. 'We all know that.'

'*He* was the one that left *us* in the lurch mid-project,' muttered Alice. 'It's his stupid fault the visitors' centre is running so far behind schedule, nothing to do with us! Another job came up and he decided that it paid better.'

'But you've not cancelled *Knit One Pour One?*' said Nell again.

Alice shook her head. 'No. I mean, I *did* think I was going to have to postpone it for a while but it's sorted now – I've got a solution!' She paused and took a deep breath. 'I can't believe Warren! What a mess.'

'It gets a bit worse than that I'm afraid, dear,' said Nell, pulling out a chair and giving her a worried look as she sat down opposite her on the other side of the scrubbed pine kitchen table.

'Do I even want to know?' said Alice, leaning her head on her hands and then peeking at Nell through her fingers.

'Well, he's been telling everyone that you've cancelled because you've run out of money… and that Arthur is a skinflint.' Nell paused, looking at her anxiously. 'Things aren't as bad as all that, are they Alice?'

Alice straightened up and shook her head. 'No. He's lying. I mean, things are tight because we're pouring everything into doing the place up bit by bit. It doesn't help that I've just discovered that Warren's spent most of the budget for the visitors' centre on a bunch of unusable, modern tat. As for dad being a skinflint-'

'Don't worry, dear, I know that bit's not true,' said Nell quickly.

'Thanks Nell,' she muttered gratefully, watching as her old friend got up to make them a pot of tea from the now squealing kettle.

Alice loved Nell – she'd always been around – and was the closest thing to a mother she'd known in a very long time. She also knew that Nell had a soft spot for her father. In fact, if pressed, she would probably put good money on the fact that Nell had been in love with Arthur Merryfield for years. But it was something that few people seemed to be aware of, and it was none of her business, so she kept her mouth shut.

'So, how's your dad coping with the whole idea of opening the vineyard up to the world again after all these years?' asked Nell, bringing the teapot and a couple of mugs over to the table.

Alice shrugged. 'I'd be lying if I said he was finding it easy. Until recently, it's all been a bit of a struggle – but when we talked about it, he agreed that it was time.'

'Well,' said Nell, a fond smile creeping over her face, 'at least he's on-side with it – even if he's finding the reality a bit tough to take.'

'Yeah. Plus – we had a bit of an unexpected visitor arrive yesterday. Jake's definitely helped matters where dad's concerned!'

'Who's Jake?' asked Nell with interest.

Alice did her best to keep the goofy grin that was threatening to break through under wraps. 'He broke down next to the bridge. He's staying in the boathouse while he gets himself sorted out,' she said.

There, that sounded nice and neutral, didn't it? She didn't need to tell Nell about the kiss or his amazing eyes or how everything just felt right with him around. Blimey, Jake had only arrived yesterday, and he had her behaving like a flippin' swooning regency heroine already. Only – well, she couldn't imagine Mr Darcy mending a boat engine.

Alice might be able to control how much she *told* Nell, but she had a sneaking suspicion that the furious blush now staining her cheeks might be all the explanation her friend needed.

Alice glanced at Nell, but she just smiled back and serenely sipped her tea. This was exactly why Alice adored Nell. She never pried, never pushed her opinion or interrogated her – even when she'd been a nightmare teenager. Nell was just a calming, lovely presence, and right now, Alice couldn't be more grateful.

Sipping at her own mug of tea, Alice started to feel calm for the first time since her ridiculous lunge at Jake. She really did just need to put that to the back of her mind for now. She was sure she'd get the chance to apologise properly later on. For now – she was on a mission – and that was what was important. She was here to talk biscuits.

Nell made the best biscuits in the village and Alice had a sneaking suspicion that they might be the essential element in pulling the gathering of nutty knitters together.

'Hey, Nell,' she said tentatively.

'Yes Alice,' said Nell, a huge smile crossing her face at the traditional opening of Alice asking her for a favour. It had happened far too many times to count over the years Nell had been playing surrogate mother to her.

'I don't suppose you'd be willing to make some biscuits for *Knit One Pour One* would you?'

'I think that could be arranged,' laughed Nell, as Alice promptly felt herself regress into a little girl asking for help with a school project. 'What type were you thinking?'

Alice paused a moment, considering the question. 'Well, your butter cookies are a *must* because frankly, they're to die for, and some double chocolate... and some raisin and almond... and-'

Nell held up her hands in mock surrender, letting out a laugh. 'Steady on there, my girl! How many people are coming? Because with that lot I could be baking all week.'

Alice pulled an apologetic face. 'Well, I'm actually not sure... especially after what you've just told me about Warren!'

Nell shook her head. 'Don't worry about that. We'll soon undo his vicious gossip. Anyway, as far as I know, most of the village were planning to come. There hasn't been anything to do here forever, what with the village hall being closed up.'

'I know,' sighed Alice. She couldn't help a spike of unease as she thought about it. They could have done something for their local community so much sooner. Still, there was no point thinking like that, was there? What was important now was making sure everything went off without a hitch.

'Your visitors' centre is going to be a lifeline for this community – mark my words,' said Nell, her voice firm.

Alice nodded. 'I hope so. I just – well... when you

spread the word that it's back on, can you make sure everyone knows that the first few weeks are going to be a bit… different?'

'Different?' laughed Nell. 'There's nothing wrong with different! Things around here are a bit slow going at the best of times – even when you live in one of the most beautiful valleys in the entire country, sometimes things need a good shake up! After all, everyone needs a bit of excitement from time to time… a bit of colour and adventure, know what I mean?'

Alice nodded. She knew what Nell meant more than she cared to admit. Yet again, she felt the pang of regret that she hadn't done more – hadn't *seen* more. She wished she'd travelled a bit. Not that it was too late, of course, not really. But Jake's stories about his travels as they'd whiled away the previous evening had made her feel that she'd missed out by staying put at the vineyard with her dad for all these years.

Things might have been so different if her mum had still been with them. Then it wouldn't have felt so much like abandoning her dad to leave the vineyard for a while. But then again – it was only recently that she'd had any urge to see the outside world.

Maybe Nell was right. Maybe it was just time for a little bit of a shake-up. After all, the winds of change seemed to have blown in with their unexpected guest. Jake had brought a breath of fresh air with him all the way down from the Scottish Isles. He was their little bit of magic. She was already dreading the moment he fixed his van and was ready to continue his adventure, leaving them behind.

CHAPTER 9

*L*ate that afternoon, Alice set off across the vineyard in search of her father. Now that everything was starting to look like it might come together for *Knit One Pour One*, she wanted to run it all past him again.

If she was being completely honest with herself, she was mildly dreading his reaction. The addition of the circus tent meant more change and disruption – and that just wasn't something her dad had ever dealt with very well. But it couldn't be helped. At least she was going to him with a solution... even if it was a slightly bonkers one.

Alice wandered along the rows of vines, all tied in neatly and tended with so much love. She was making her way up the side of one of the slopes that faced the river. This field had always been one of her dad's favourite spots at this time of day. She was hoping that she'd find him working at the top of the hill, enjoying the evening sunshine and admiring the view down the valley as she had so many times before.

Arthur Merryfield had spent over twenty years focusing on the land - and the vines - and the wine. Ever since he'd lost Alice's mum, this had been his sole focus – barring the tiny part of himself he kept available for her.

Sure enough, as she crested the hill, Alice spotted him sitting on the bench right at the top, gazing at the river. The late rays of sunshine were painting the wide bends of the Bamton a molten gold.

'Alice!' he said in surprise. 'How lovely!'

'Hi dad,' she said, giving him a smile and dropping down onto the bench next to him.

'Everything okay?' he asked. 'Unusual to see you up here at this time of day.'

'Everything's fine. I just thought I'd fill you in on what's going on... if I'm not interrupting?'

'Hardly!' he laughed. 'But I can never get enough of this view.'

Alice nodded. 'It is pretty special.'

'It was your mum's favourite spot in the whole place, you know?'

Alice swallowed hard and nodded. 'I can see why.'

'Me too,' Arthur sighed. 'Anyway – what's this update?'

'Well... you know I've been a bit worried about how

to run *Knit One Pour One* without the visitors' centre ready to use?'

Arthur nodded but didn't say anything.

'Jake's come up with a solution.' Urgh, here came the hard bit. There was no way her dad was going to embrace the whole idea of using a tent.

'And?' prompted her dad, looking amused for some reason.

'He's got a massive circus tent!'

'Of course he has!' chuckled her dad. 'That's such a brilliant idea!'

Alice raised her eyebrows in surprise. 'You like it?'

'Of course I do,' he laughed. 'Don't you?'

Alice nodded quickly. 'I think it's going to be brilliant.'

She paused for a moment, trying to get her head around the fact that her dad suddenly seemed to be open to change after years of being so stubbornly against it.

'Nell's agreed to make biscuits and there should actually be quite a crowd there.' She paused again, wondering whether she should tell him about Warren's latest, delightful bout of lies, but swiftly decided to keep that to herself for now.

'You know,' said her dad, staring out at the gorgeous view below them, 'it's going to be like old times again. When your mum was alive, we used to have people around the place all the time. She loved to entertain.'

Alice nodded quietly.

'Where are you planning to pitch the tent?' he asked curiously.

'Jake suggested the long lawn in the courtyard behind the visitors' centre. Obviously, we'll need to clear it before then, but it seems like the perfect place.'

'That's where we used to hold the parties when you were little, you know,' he said, smiling at her. 'I guess you probably don't remember them?'

Alice nodded again. 'I do,' she said, her voice breaking. She quickly cleared her throat. 'I remember you and mum dancing on the lawn. And I remember Lionel being there too sometimes.'

The place had been so happy back then – when the vineyard was alive - a thriving place full of friendship and laughter. It was as though it had been asleep ever since.

'Good times,' said her dad, his voice gruff.

Alice glanced at him, worried that this conversation was upsetting him. Perhaps he *was* struggling with all this change after all.

'I'm really sorry, Alice,' he sighed.

'Why?' she said, a lump of fear lodging somewhere in her stomach at his sudden change in mood.

'I'm sorry you got stuck in this old place with me. It must have been so hard growing up without your mum. I know I didn't make it easy for you – being distant and focused on keeping everything together. I should have travelled with you – but there was always something to do here, even if it was just making sure that everything remained the same.'

Alice frowned. Reaching over, she laid her hand on top of his where it rested on the bench and squeezed his fingers tightly. She wanted to say something to reassure him. He'd never said anything like this before, but he clearly hadn't finished yet.

'I know that I'm an old stick in the mud,' he huffed, 'but I thought it was for the best. Keeping things the same. Keeping your mum's memory alive here. I still do. I don't regret it.'

Alice shook her head. 'Dad, if it wasn't for the way you've protected this valley, it would be full of holiday homes and terrible flats by now. Besides – I had the most magical childhood here with you. I loved it. I still do. Of course I missed mum and I always will, but I've loved living here with you.'

Arthur shifted on the bench and Alice looked at him, wanting to make sure that he was listening to her and really taking in what she was saying.

'Really?' he asked.

Alice swallowed hard when she saw that his eyes were swimming with tears, even though he was smiling at her like she was the most precious thing in the entire universe.

'Every single second,' said Alice.

'Come here,' said Arthur, his arms open wide. Alice slid up the bench towards her father, and he wrapped both arms around her in a huge cuddle. Tears began to trickle down her cheeks, but she didn't make a move to wipe them away.

Alice stayed sitting right next to her dad on the bench as they watched the sun begin to set over the valley. Arthur's arm was tight around her, and for the first time in years, she rested her head against his shoulder and snuggled into his side.

'You know,' said Arthur quietly, 'your mum would have been proud of you for sticking by me all these years. And even prouder for opening my eyes to the fact that we need to make some changes around here.'

'Thanks dad,' said Alice, knowing that this was his way of telling her that everything was okay. That they were on track and he was on her side. It meant the world to her.

'You know,' said Arthur again, 'given that the sun's going down, I would suggest that we head back towards the house. It must be well past six again – we're late for supper!'

Alice let out a laugh. Because he was right. It seemed like the old rules they'd lived by for so many years were starting to fall apart. Maybe it was for the best.

Somehow, she had a sneaking suspicion she knew who to blame - or maybe to thank - for all the changes that were happening.

.   .   .

They arrived in the farmhouse kitchen twenty minutes later to find that both Jake and Basil had beaten them to it. Basil was spark-out, stretched full length in front of the lovely warm stove. Jake was bustling around the kitchen.

'I hope you don't mind that I let myself in!' he said. 'I thought you had a strict 6pm dinner time – and I couldn't find either of you... so I thought I'd start cooking!'

'In that case,' said Arthur, going to wash his hands with a gritty cake of yellow soap at the sink, 'we definitely don't mind! I'm ravenous!'

Alice bent to stroke Basil's head, earning a couple of solid tail-thumps in greeting. She was finding it rather hard to look at Jake as he moved so easily around their kitchen. After all, it was the first time she'd seen him since pouncing on him that morning.

Maybe she should beat a hasty retreat and leave the two men to it? It would be a good idea if it wasn't for the fact that her stomach was growling fairly insistently. Chiding herself for being a complete coward, she straightened up and went over to the sink to wash her own hands.

'What's on the menu?' she asked lightly, glad her voice didn't sound as strange as she was feeling.

'Pasta with a basic tomato sauce,' said Jake. 'I'm not much of a cook, but I thought that was a pretty safe bet. Plus, I didn't want to raid your cupboards too much without asking!'

'For future reference – you're free to raid away to your heart's content!' laughed Arthur. 'But pasta sounds perfect to me!'

Alice glanced over to find that Jake already had a huge pot of spaghetti on the boil, and was in the process of whizzing up a herby sauce.

'Blimey,' said Arthur, looking impressed, 'not even out of a jar! Alice, I think you'd better marry this guy before he runs away!'

Alice felt her face flush, wishing she'd followed her gut and done a runner while she could.

'Right, I'll just heat this through and we'll be ready,' said Jake, clearly deciding that the safest bet was to ignore Arthur's joke entirely, for which Alice was intensely grateful.

'I'll grab some bowls,' she said, glad of the excuse to turn her back on the other two for a moment as she rummaged in one of the under-counter cupboards.

A few minutes later, the three of them were stationed at the table in front of heaped bowls of fragrant pasta. Silence descended as they tucked in – the kind of silence that only happened when everyone was famished and the food far too delicious to pause in the act of stuffing your face. It was only when Basil's deep, rumbling snores started to echo around the kitchen that they all began to giggle.

'Not the neatest of meals, I'm afraid,' muttered Jake with an apologetic frown as he dabbed at a splodge of red that had just flicked from his fork onto the white tablecloth.

'Don't worry about it, lad,' said Arthur, lifting his bowl briefly to reveal a full halo of splatters around his dish.

'Oh my goodness, dad!' laughed Alice.

'Bet you've got one too,' he grinned.

Alice lifted her bowl and sure enough, even though she thought she'd been pretty careful, there was a ring of tomato-coloured dots on the cloth in front of her. 'Oops,' she laughed.

'I think Arthur's in the lead, though,' said Jake with a smile.

'Let's see yours, then,' said Arthur.

'Are we really turning this into a competition?' demanded Alice.

'Too bloomin' right!' said Arthur.

'Okay, you're on,' said Jake. 'But first – what's the prize for the winner?'

'Winner gets to choose desert?' suggested Alice with a laugh.

'Good choice!' nodded Arthur. 'Now then Jake, let's see what you've got!'

Jake lifted his plate.

'Not bad,' said Alice, 'but I'd say dad wins this round.'

Jake nodded, laughing at the delighted look on Arthur's face. Alice grinned between the two of them. She'd never seen her father this happy – or this alive.

He was like a new man – one that was at least ten years younger. Sure, he might need a new haircut and perhaps change his sweater to complete the transformation... but maybe she'd keep that to herself for the time being.

'Chocolate ice cream,' said Arthur, his voice as determined and excited as a six-year-old's.

'You, sir, are a genius,' laughed Jake with an approving nod.

CHAPTER 10

*A*lice couldn't help the ball of nerves that had built up in her chest. The sun was out, the sky was blue... and she'd quite happily turn tail and hide back underneath her duvet for the rest of the day. It was yet another beautiful morning, and she was on her way down to the boathouse to have a chat with Jake about what was going to happen next.

Not about the kiss. Nope - not that. Neither of them had mentioned it last night, even though it had been like a massive elephant in the room between them. Still, she was quite happy to carry on pretending it had never happened. Maybe it was for the best.

Maybe she was busy building it up into something way more important than it actually was. Perhaps it hadn't meant that much to him. Not that it had meant that much to her either of course. After all, she *had* only just met him. It had just been a strange moment.

One she should put behind her. Oh crap, here she went again, tying herself up in knots.

Alice paused on the path, doing her best to calm down. She needed to get her head straightened out. She stared at the mass of wildflowers growing along the bank. They looked like they were trying to outdo each other in the morning sun. The effect was gorgeous. She took in a long, deep breath and let it out slowly.

See, she could be calm. She could manage to have a chat with Jake without obsessing, couldn't she? Because she really needed to talk to him about starting work on the visitors' centre, as well as getting the tent in place.

The three of them had had such a wonderful meal together the night before that she hadn't wanted to bring the conversation around to work. Not when her dad was so relaxed. So she'd avoided anything that might break the relaxed vibe, and determinedly stayed away from topics like building work, ex-boyfriends... kissing Jake...

Nope. She wasn't going to let her head go there again!

The sound of a very unhappy engine struggling to turn over met her ears, and she continued along the path towards the boathouse. Clearly Jake was trying to get the van going. For just a second, it sounded like it was going to catch, but then it died again.

Alice breathed a sigh of relief. She knew she shouldn't, but she suddenly realised that her life would look very different when Jake left. Not that she'd admit it to anyone, of course, but she would rather that Jake was stuck here with them for as long as possible.

Alice let out a gentle snort. What was she even thinking? She didn't know anything about him. Not really. She had no idea what his plans were or where he was going to go next. Maybe he was just planning on driving around forever, never calling anywhere home – or at least, not for very long.

There was another reluctant grumble from a very unhappy engine, followed by a mechanical squeal - and then silence. That really hadn't sounded good!

There was a mechanic who worked over at Bamton Motors who'd probably be able to help Jake out – maybe she should give Jake his details. But then again, maybe she shouldn't. The longer the van was having problems, the longer Jake would stay here with them. Uh oh – now there was a conundrum to add to her already frazzled nerves!

As she rounded the bend in the path and the boathouse appeared in front of her, she could see that Jake was bent over the van. Practically his entire top half was lost to the dark cave under the open bonnet. Alice paused for a moment, unable to stop herself from admiring the view. She jumped as a stream of swear-words brought her back to reality with a bump. That *really* wasn't sounding promising.

Alice wandered over towards Jake. He was so engrossed in what he was doing that she eventually gave a little cough to get his attention – she didn't want

to make him jump and clonk his head on the bonnet –
that wouldn't help matters at all!

'Alice!' said Jake, straightening up and staring at her
in surprise. 'I'm so sorry for the language – I didn't
realise you were there!'

Alice smiled as she watched him wipe his oily hands
on a rag he had draped over his shoulder. 'Don't worry
about that!' she said. 'It didn't sound very promising
though...'

Jake shook his head, an unfamiliar look of frustration etched on his tanned face.

'The poor old thing has done some pretty heavy
miles in the last few months. A whole bunch of ferry
rides between the islands and too many coastal roads
definitely haven't helped matters. All that salty spray
combined with bumpy, twisty roads have caused abso-
lute havoc. It really needs a complete strip-down and
rebuild by the look of things.'

'Oh dear,' said Alice lightly, doing her best not to
sound pleased by the news. 'So, how long would that
take?'

'At least a few weeks,' sighed Jake. 'And that depends
on if I can get my hands on the parts. Probably a lot
longer, though.'

That sounded like fantastic news to Alice, and once
again she considered not telling him about the guys at
Bamton Motors - because she was pretty sure they'd be
able to help him source what he needed. She couldn't
bring herself to be quite as mean as that, though.

'There's a really good mechanic over at Bamton Motors – just up the road near Little Bamton. I bet he'd be able to help out with the work… or maybe just find you the parts you're after?'

Jake smiled at her gratefully. 'Thanks Alice, that's brilliant – I'll bear them in mind. I'll keep tinkering around with it myself for a few more days though. I don't really have the money to pay anyone to do the work for me at the moment, so I need to see if I can just patch her up for now.'

Alice nodded, a rush of relief going through her.

'We've been through a lot together,' said Jake, patting the side of the van fondly. 'I've been sleeping in the back on and off for years now. It's become home for me.'

'Where was home before?' asked Alice curiously as she watched him lean back into the engine. 'I mean, where abouts are your family?'

'Bit of a long story, that one,' said Jake.

Alice couldn't tell from the tone of his voice if she'd just put her foot in it or not. She shifted her weight uncomfortably. Not being able to see his face, she wasn't sure if she should quickly change the subject.

'They're kind of spread all over the country,' he continued, letting her off the hook. 'I've got lots of half brothers and sisters and stepbrothers and sisters and cousins and uncles scattered all over the place. To be honest, it's all a bit difficult to keep up with!'

'Wow,' said Alice. 'I can't imagine what it must be

like to have such a big family. It's just been me and dad for almost as far back as I can remember.'

Jake straightened up and shrugged. 'There are so many of them that I'm not particularly close to any of them, if that makes sense?'

Alice nodded. She wasn't sure she really understood what he meant, but she didn't want him to stop talking. At long last, she was actually getting a glimpse into his life.

'Anyway, I set off on my own several years ago. I don't really have a specific place that's home – other than the van.' He paused for a moment, running a thoughtful thumb along a patch of blistered paint on the edge of the bonnet. 'I'd like to one day though. Maybe not yet. Maybe… maybe later.'

'I'm sorry,' Alice said quickly, 'I didn't mean to pry.'

Jake shook his head. 'Don't worry,' he smiled. 'I mean, you don't really know anything about me – it's natural you want to know *something* about the random guy you found trespassing!'

Alice grinned at him.

'You know,' said Jake, 'I think you've been incredibly generous to let me stay here. And I'm really grateful.'

Alice shook her head. 'I'm the one who's grateful.' She quickly stopped herself. Urgh, if she didn't watch out, she was going to start gushing. She was bordering on being totally embarrassing as it was.

'Hey,' said Jake, 'it's such a lovely day, why don't we bring those chairs out here?'

'Chairs?' said Alice, reeling slightly at the sudden change of subject.

'Yeah, those old wooden ones that need a bit of work that I uncovered when I was tidying up. I'm not sure how many you're going to need, but we could give them a good clean and maybe a bit of sandpapering?'

'I'm not sure how many we're going to need either,' said Alice, frowning with worry.

'Well, I've divided them up,' said Jake, slamming the van's bonnet down before leading her inside the boathouse and over to the pile of old wooden furniture. 'There are about a dozen that are fairly sound. Maybe we should start with them, then we can work on the others if we have the time?'

'Great!' said Alice. Following his lead, she grabbed a couple of chairs from the pile and hauled them out into the sunshine. 'They're going to need painting when we're done,' she added, peering at the weather-stained wood.

'Not to worry – we've got that covered too!' said Jake with a grin, indicating for her to follow him back inside.

In a dark corner right at the back of the building, Jake had stacked up about two dozen old paint tins.

'There's bound to be something usable in the bottom of some of these, isn't there?' he said.

Alice shrugged. 'Only one way to find out!'

'Roger that,' laughed Jake. 'Give me two secs.' He dashed out towards the van again and was back in two seconds brandishing a pair of very long screwdrivers. 'Here,' he said, handing one over.

Alice dug the tip of the screwdriver into the groove at the top of the nearest paint can. With a bit of a grunt, she levered the lid off. It took some effort as it was partially welded closed by ancient, crispy paint - but she was well rewarded for her efforts.

'There's half a tin of lovely dark red here,' she said triumphantly.

'And I've got a little bit of sky blue that isn't solid. The dark green is one for the bin though.'

'Shame!' laughed Alice, levering her way into another tin. 'This one too – not that it's any loss as it's only magnolia.'

Jake grinned. 'The most boring paint colour in the universe. The rest are awesome though!' he said, looking at the kaleidoscope of pots they'd already amassed.

Alice nodded. 'Dad always was a bit of an eccentric when it came to paint colours.'

'They're all marine paint,' said Jake in surprise.

'Yeah – half the farmhouse is coated in the stuff! That bright red was for the door on the second landing. And we used the sky blue on the window frames of the winery office.'

'Blimey,' said Jake. 'It's like a history of the vineyard told in paint tins!'

'Quite the adventure, eh?' Alice grinned at him.

'Do you reckon it'll do for the chairs though?' he asked.

Alice nodded in excitement. She adored the idea of them being painted all colours of the rainbow – each of them with tiny, colourful links to the history of her home.

CHAPTER 11

*A*lice straightened her spine and gazed at the five chairs she'd already painted. She grinned and then took in a long, deep breath, trying not to get too high on paint fumes while she was at it.

Jake had gone off with her father in his old Land Rover about an hour ago. Their plan was to hunt down a few things for the work on the visitors' centre. Jake had left Basil behind with Alice as it had proved to be impossible to prize him away from his patch of sunlight in front of the boathouse.

Alice had thought that she'd find it a bit annoying, having to keep an eye on him all afternoon - but she'd quickly found that she enjoyed Basil's company. He'd quickly abandoned his snoozing spot once Jake had disappeared, and it was funny how quickly she'd become used to having a slightly grumpy, hairy shadow pottering around behind her and demanding the occasional tickle.

Alice was having a brilliant time working on the chairs – and as proof, she had an entire rainbow of paint smudges and splatters all over her dungarees. Frankly, she liked the multi-colour additions, and she had the feeling she'd cherish them as a reminder of working alongside Jake. Not that it was a bad thing that he'd gone off with her father for a while – it had given her the chance to get her feet back on the ground a bit.

'Who am I kidding, eh boy?' she sighed, running her fingers lightly over Basil's ears as the little dog closed his eyes. 'Even when your dad's not around, I'm daydreaming about him!'

Basil thumped his tail lazily on the grass and then slid down onto his back, legs in the air and an idiotic grin on his face as he begged for a belly rub. Alice started to laugh and gave in immediately. Crikey, it wasn't just Jake she was going to miss when he did finally manage to get his old van started again.

Suddenly, she felt Basil stiffen under her hand, and a low, rumbling tremor ran through his body.

What on earth?

Basil's low growl intensified and he righted himself, jumping to his feet just as Alice felt an uncomfortable prickle start on the back of her neck. Shivering slightly, she straightened up and turned around.

Huh. Talk about an ill wind appearing out of

nowhere. Warren was walking down the path towards her. Urgh, well that was one way to ruin a perfect day.

Basil promptly placed himself squarely in front of her, facing the newcomer with his tail low. He clearly hated Warren on sight. Alice couldn't help but admire his excellent judge of character. Basil was definitely better at it than her.

'Just don't bite him,' she muttered under her breath. 'You don't know where he's been!'

'Ali!' said Warren, spreading his arms wide, grinning at her.

Alice shuddered. She hated that nickname. It just wasn't her – it was some new thing he'd decided on and wouldn't drop no matter how many times she insisted her name was Alice.

'What do you want, Warren?' she said, her voice flat. She didn't particularly want to pick a fight with him – she didn't have the energy for all that right now – but neither was she going to pretend that everything was okay between them. Because it really, *really* wasn't. He could act all sweetness and light if he wanted to, but it didn't change the fact that he was a giant douchebag who'd left her in the lurch.

'No need to be like that,' he said, his voice coming out in a snidey whine.

Basil let out another growl and took a solid step towards Warren, who mirrored by taking a step backwards, glancing nervously down at the angry dog.

'There's every reason for me to be like that,' said

Alice. 'You buggered off mid-job and left me to pick up the pieces.'

'Nah,' said Warren, shaking his head and tearing his eyes away from Basil to look pleadingly at her. 'You've got it all wrong. I didn't *think* you fully understood our arrangement. We discussed all this right at the beginning. Don't you remember?'

'Enlighten me,' she said, crossing her arms and raising an eyebrow. How dare he come and ruin her lovely, colourful day with all his bullshit?

'This is just a misunderstanding,' he said with a shrug. 'No bother. Anyway, me and the lads should be able to be back on-site in about a fortnight.'

'Is that right?' she said, her voice dripping with sarcasm. Sadly it was totally lost on Warren. Had the guy always been such a total and utter plank, she wondered?

'Yeah,' he said. 'But we'll need a good wodge of cash upfront for the materials you're going to need.'

Alice bit her tongue, willing herself not to completely lose her shit as a swell of anger threatened to overtake her. She'd just about managed to get it under control when Warren went and put the nail in his own coffin.

'I mean, I know your old man's a total tight-arse, but we can't work with thin air you know!'

Alice wasn't sure whether it was her or Basil who let out the loud growl that made Warren take another step backwards away from the pair of them. By the approving glance Basil shot at her however, she'd hazard a guess that it had been her.

'Don't you *dare* say anything like that about my dad again,' she spat.

'Come on Ali, I-'

'My *name* is Alice,' she said, her voice low and tight as she tried to control herself. 'My father is one of the most generous men I've ever met. Y*ou*, however, are a sleazy little asshat.'

'What the hell?' said Warren, shooting a hurt look at her.

'You've already spent my entire budget – on all the wrong things. You've *completely* ignored the plans we agreed when you started the job.'

'To be fair,' said Warren, 'I was just trying to save you time and money. You don't really know what you're talking about when it comes to this sort of stuff – you said so yourself.'

Alice snorted. She had said no such thing.

'My way's better. You've got to see that. Way more modern. The PVC windows will last, and plasterboard means all that mess inside is covered. Gone.'

Alice shook her head. 'It's an old building Warren. It needs to be treated with respect.'

'God, you sound exactly like your dad sometimes, you know that?'

'And what's wrong with that?' she said, her voice rising in anger again.

'That silly old sod could have made a fortune a

thousand times over if he'd just listened to me. He should have scrapped those stupid vines years ago.'

Alice's jaw dropped. Either Warren had become even worse since she'd come to her senses and dumped him, or she'd managed to block out the memory of just how greedy, grabbing and obnoxious he could be.

'As if he'd ever do that,' she said.

'That's the problem, Ali,' said Warren, his voice going gentle as he took a step forward, half extending a hand as if he was about to try to take hers. Basil let out a low grumble, baring his teeth. Warren promptly backed away again. 'You deserve someone who'll make him see sense. He's holding you back – and I think I can help.'

Alice opened her mouth as if to respond but found there were no words waiting to come out. What on earth was this idiot saying? That he wanted her back?

'I've been talking to this property developer about the potential of the vineyard,' he continued. 'There could be millions of pounds in it!'

Alice shook her head slowly, staring at him, barely able to believe that *this* was why he was back. The same old rubbish he'd been spouting for years – only now she could see it for what it was. He didn't care about *her*. All he cared about was the potential windfall. Though *why* he thought that any of it would ever come his way was beyond her.

'Come on, Ali. If you could just see sense and get

with the program – we could all be rich!' said Warren, his eyes gleaming.

The guy was deluded.

'Don't shake your head,' he continued. 'You know I'm right. You've been living in the past. I don't know how you've both survived in that knackered old house for so long. You can't even heat it properly!'

'I-' Alice finally opened her mouth to tell him exactly what she thought of him, but Warren was on a roll and cut her off.

'You should move in with me,' he said, triumphantly. 'Come and live in a proper house with double glazing and central heating and see how the other half live.'

'No,' said Alice, pulling a face.

'What do you mean, "no"?' said Warren.

'I mean – no!' said Alice, letting out an unamused laugh. 'Why the hell would I do that? We're not together anymore. I don't even *like* you. *Why* you'd think I'd ever agree to live with you is beyond me.'

'I'm sure we could find some kind of retirement place for your dad if that's what you're worried about,' he sighed.

'Okay, that's it. I'd like you to leave,' said Alice.

Basil glanced up at her and then turned back to stare at Warren, clearly waiting for the slightest hint that his services were needed.

'Well,' said Warren, looking like someone had

pooped in his sandpit, 'if that's your attitude, I'll take all my things with me!'

'What things?' snapped Alice. 'There aren't any *things!* You made sure you took it all when you buggered off to that other job.'

'Fine – the materials I left behind then.'

Alice shook her head. 'They're not yours to take. I paid for all of that and I've got the receipts to prove it.'

She didn't really *need* any of the rubbish he'd spent her precious budget on, but it might come in handy for some future project. Besides, it was worth its weight in gold right now just to see the look of pure fury on Warren's face.

'You're making a huge mistake, you know!' he said, sounding decidedly mean all of a sudden.

'Just leave,' sighed Alice.

Warren went to take a step forward, but Basil had clearly had enough and let out a low bark, planting his feet firmly, his fur bristling with anger. Warren glanced down, paused for a moment and then turned on his heel and stomped off towards the main drive.

Basil promptly gave chase, following him all the way down the path, clearly making sure he was actually leaving. Alice heard him let out a volley of angry barks as he stood stiffly, hackles up, watching the unwelcome visitor disappear from view.

When he was certain Warren had definitely gone, Basil turned and trotted proudly back towards Alice, his little tail wagging frantically.

'Yes, you're a very good boy,' she laughed, dropping to her knees and making a fuss of him, kissing his bent nose. 'My good brave boy!'

Alice wrapped her arms around Basil's sturdy little body for a moment, soaking in his comforting warmth as she tried to let the icky feeling of Warren's presence leave her.

She couldn't believe he thought that he could just waltz back to the vineyard and expect everything to be okay! The man was clearly living in some kind of deranged, cloud-cuckoo-land.

'I'm okay, boy, I'm okay,' she laughed, as Basil stuck his nose in her ear and snuffled.

She wasn't really okay, though. Warren had managed to shake her more than she cared to admit. He'd always been so eager to encourage them both to develop the vineyard - in fact, it was one of the reasons they'd split up. He'd become more and more persistent, and she knew she was nearing breaking point.

Warren had then made the fatal mistake of asking her if she would end up inheriting the place when Arthur died. Alice had lost her temper and they'd come very close to splitting up – but Warren had backed down and they'd called an uneasy truce. She'd thought the subject was over and done with after that - but she hadn't given Warren credit for just how bloody-minded he could be.

Several very rocky weeks later, she'd discovered that he'd simply moved his offensive from her over to her dad. Arthur hadn't liked Warren much to start with, but the fact that he was pressuring him about this most sensitive of subjects had made sure it was a done deal – Arthur loathed him.

Still, her dad had wrestled with himself and hadn't told Alice about what was going on for several weeks. They never kept secrets from each other for very long though, and it had all come pouring out one evening.

That had been the final straw for Alice and she confronted Warren. He'd said that as she didn't seem to care about what was best for her family, someone else needed to act. According to him, he'd been doing it "with the old man's best interests at heart."

That had not gone down as well as he'd expected it to. She ended their relationship there and then.

'I should never have asked him back here, should I?' she whispered into Basil's ear, earning herself a soggy lick on the cheek.

The thing was, builders were hard to find around here – the decent ones were already booked well in advance, and old places were being done up left, right and centre. She'd bumped into Warren by chance and he'd offered to do it for them. Like an idiot - she'd agreed.

By that point, she'd managed to convince herself that she'd been too hard on him – overreacting to his offers of help because she was oversensitive. Losing her mum had made her incredibly protective of her dad… and her home. She'd thought that perhaps this was the perfect opportunity to heal the rift between herself and Warren – to at least become friends again.

Warren had never once taken the job seriously. He'd not treated her like a paying client, and by the time he cleared off again, Alice had realised that it had all been a part of some weird plan to get them back together. It was blatantly obvious that he wasn't actually interested in her, though. He just wanted to get his foot back in the door back at the vineyard. His ultimate aim was clearly to talk them into developing the place… and getting his hands on as much of the cash as possible.

Well, there was no chance in hell she was ever going to let that happen. Alice had no intention of ever letting Warren set foot on the place again.

CHAPTER 12

*B*asil might have done the job and seen Warren off the property, but unfortunately, he'd managed to get inside Alice's head. She soon found that she had too much pent-up anger and frustration to go back to the relatively chilled job of painting the wooden chairs. She needed something that would soak up all the angry energy that she hadn't unleashed on the idiot.

'Come on Basil,' she said. She hastily placed the cover back on the tin of paint she'd been using and popped her brush in to soak so that it didn't harden in the sunshine. 'I've got a better plan.'

She patted her thigh and Basil trotted after her as she made her way towards her dad's workshop. Letting herself into the cool, dark space, she took in a deep breath, letting the familiar scent of wood and carefully oiled tools calm her jangled nerves. Right – it was time to choose her weapon!

She gently lifted an ancient, long-handled slash-hook down from its spot on the wall. The curved blade gleamed. It should be perfect! She grabbed some loppers and a pair of thick gloves for good measure and headed back out into the sunshine.

Wandering around to the visitors' centre with Basil hot on her heels, she threw a filthy look at the pile of unwanted materials that Jake had discovered. Sod it, she didn't want to think about that particular problem right now.

She skirted around the outside of the building and passed under the old stone arch, coming to stand at the edge of the little wilderness that used to be a lawn. This was where they were planning to pitch the tent for *Knit One Pour One,* but before they could do that, it needed some serious attention.

Alice eyeballed the dense patch of brambles with relish. If she was looking for a bit of anger therapy – she couldn't get much better than this! It was so overgrown that some of the bramble stems were like small trees, and she could see prickles in amongst the tangle that were the size of fish hooks. At least the stinging nettles hadn't really got going on this patch… she had to be thankful for small mercies!

Pulling on the thick pair of long leather gloves, she quickly checked that Basil was safe and sound out of the way. With his guard duty done, the little dog had flopped down next to the visitors' centre stone wall and was already snoring in a patch of warm sunshine. Perfect! Alice stepped forward, ready to take on her thorny adversary.

After just twenty minutes, she was sweating buckets. She had dirt and leaves and goodness knows what in her hair, filthy smears across her face, and a good few scratches here and there too. She was already beginning to feel better.

Alice had already managed to make some pretty good progress, and there was a growing pile of hacked and chopped brambles at the far end of the space. She'd barrow them away later or, even better, maybe she'd pile them up with some of the bits of scrap wood she'd unearthed and make a bonfire.

Alice paused and rested the hook against the stone wall. Then she pulled off one of her gloves and wiped her hand across her sweaty face. Blimey – not only was this excellent therapy, but it was a full-body work out too!

'There you are!'

Alice spun around to find her dad and Jake heading towards her.

'Wow Alice,' said Jake, looking impressed, 'you've made a serious inroad! I had no idea you were planning on tackling this lot today!'

Alice smiled at him and then noticed the curious expression on her father's face. She should have known she wouldn't be able to sneak anything past him – he simply knew her too well.

'Warren stopped by,' she muttered.

'Ah,' said Arthur, a little frown appearing between his bushy eyebrows, 'enough said!'

'It's okay,' said Alice with a shrug, 'Basil saw him off for me.' She smiled down at Basil who was getting his ears tickled by Jake.

'You been playing guard dog, eh boy?' Jake laughed.

Basil thumped his tail before flopping back down onto the sun-warmed flagstones near the stone wall, instantly closing his eyes for another snooze.

'Right,' said Arthur, 'give us two seconds to grab some tools and we'll both join you, eh Jake?'

Jake nodded with a grin. 'Absolutely!'

'Can't let you have all the fun!' said Arthur, over his shoulder as the pair of them head back in the direction of the workshop.

Having poured all of her anger into hacking away at the bramble jungle on her own, Alice was now more than happy to have some company. All three of them set to work and piled up the mess into a huge bonfire as they went. Arthur had quickly agreed that there wasn't any point in them struggling to move it when they could enjoy a fire instead.

Alice had always liked bonfires. Just the idea of it was bringing memories of her childhood flooding back in – of working alongside her dad to care for the vineyard. Just the two of them – just the way she'd loved it.

She didn't care what that idiot Warren had said – her dad was her hero, and she treasured the time they'd spent together. The fact that she still loved working alongside him in the home that meant so much to both of them... well, that was worth fighting for.

The sky was already beginning to dim by the time they'd finished hacking down the last of the brambles and piling them up onto what was now promising to be quite an epic fire.

'Blimey – talk about a day disappearing in a blink of an eye!' laughed Jake, leaning on the long-handled fork he'd just been using to toss the last of the spiny brash on top of the pile.

'That's what happens when you're having fun, eh?' said Arthur, fanning his face with his flat cap.

'You know, we've all managed to miss supper again!' laughed Alice. 'I'm ravenous!'

'Well, that's music to my ears,' came a voice from behind them.

'Nell!' cheered Arthur, turning to find their old friend appearing around the corner of the old stone building, led proudly by Basil who'd mooched off some time earlier in search of one of his comfy snoozing spots.

Alice grinned at Nell and peered hopefully at the Tupperware box she was holding.

'I come bearing biscuits!' said Nell. 'I was just about to leave them on your doorstep when this little monkey appeared, so I guessed there must be someone around here somewhere. Looks like you've all been busy?'

'Biscuits?' said Jake with a groan of longing.

'You've appeared just in the nick of time, Nell!' laughed Alice. 'This is Jake – who I was telling you about – and this is Basil. Jake – this is Nell Fernsby.'

'Lovely to meet you, Nell,' said Jake with a wide smile.

'Now, what did we do to deserve biscuits?' asked Arthur.

'They're samples to see which ones Alice wants for the knit night. But I can see you're all busy,' she added quickly, looking from Alice's hook to Jake's fork. 'I'll just leave them with you and get out of your way.'

'Nonsense,' said Arthur. 'We were just about to knock off and burn this lot if you'd like to join us?'

Alice watched a soft smile spread over Nell's face. 'Okay,' she said, 'I'd like that.'

'Wonderful. Right – you two finish up here, and we'll go and get some chairs?' said Arthur, taking the box of biscuits from Nell and setting them down on a wall out of Basil's curious reach. 'Those better still be there when we get back, Jake!' he added with a laugh, catching Jake's look, which was about as longing as his dog's.

'Aw,' said Jake, sticking his bottom lip out and making Alice laugh.

'Shall we use the new chairs?' said Arthur. 'We can nip down to the boathouse and collect four?'

Alice shook her head. 'They'll still be tacky – that stuff takes forever to dry. I don't think anyone really wants a bright red bottom!'

'Right you are, fair point!' laughed Arthur. 'I've got some old, folding camp chairs in my workshop some-where. We'll go and find them.'

Alice watched her father lead Nell away from the newly-cleared patch of ground. As they disappeared around the corner, she felt a swarm of butterflies rise up in her chest. She was alone with Jake again… and they *still* hadn't mentioned anything about that kiss.

Alice suddenly felt the need to explain to Jake about Warren. She didn't want him thinking that there was still anything going on between them… nor any chance of it, come to that! Not that it would make a difference to Jake – he clearly wasn't that bothered either way - but she couldn't bear the idea of him getting the wrong end of the stick.

'Penny for them?' said Jake, gathering the various tools together and making sure that they were carefully stacked up against the old stone wall, far away from the bonfire.

'I was just thinking that I need to explain to you about Warren,' she said.

Huh. That had come out way more bluntly than she'd intended. Still, it was probably best to give him the "no-frills" version.

Jake stared at her for a moment, looking surprised, then shrugged. 'It's none of my business.'

Alice felt her little swarm of butterflies drop to the floor.

Oh. Well, that told her.

She turned away from Jake, wanting to hide her face in case her disappointment was as obvious on the outside as it felt on the inside. Just as she went to step away from him, she felt a gentle tug on her arm.

'It's not my business,' he repeated, pulling her around to face him, 'I'd *like* it to be, though.'

Jake's eyes dropped to her mouth, and for just a second Alice felt every cell in her body lean in towards him as his calloused fingers brushed against hers.

'Got them!'

Arthur's voice over near the arch made them spring apart, and like a pair of guilty teenagers, they turned to watch him lead Nell towards them. Alice felt her grubby face flush with heat as Jake's fingers brushed hers again for just a second.

'Haven't you got that thing lit yet?' her dad demanded as he carried a pair of chairs towards them.

'Don't tell me you've eaten all those biscuits already?' said Nell, raising an eyebrow at Alice. 'The face on you – I've known you too long not to know when you're hiding something, Miss Merryfield!'

Alice winced and shook her head. Trust her old friend to clock the shifty look on her face.

'I was just going to tell Jake about Warren,' she sighed.

Arthur promptly shook his head. 'No need to ruin a lovely evening talking about that waste of space.'

Her dad's voice was firm but incredibly kind, and Alice smiled at him. She knew she should be grateful to him for sparing her the awkward conversation about an epically failed relationship, but why did they have to choose that *exact* moment to reappear?!

She shot a quick look at Jake, but he was already helping Nell to set up her camp chair. Whatever *might* have just been about to happen would have to wait.

'Let's get this fire going,' she said with a sigh.

'Here you go!' said Arthur, handing a huge, steaming mug of hot chocolate to Alice. He and Nell had already brought down a round of cheese toasties for them all. Nell had absolutely refused to let them delve straight into the biscuits when she'd learned they hadn't had their tea and had insisted on preparing something delicious for them.

Nell and Arthur had just made another pitstop up to the house and returned bearing all things warm and cosy. Arthur had made a round of his famous hot chocolates topped with ridiculous amounts of cream and marshmallows, and Nell had gathered an armful of cosy blankets to ward off the tickly breeze that had started up as the daylight faded.

'Thanks, Arthur!' said Jake with a grin, accepting a large red mug and then smiling up at Nell as she

BETH RAIN

draped a knitted, patchwork blanket over his legs.
'Blimey, the royal treatment.'

As if she'd known Jake forever rather than just a few
hours, Nell patted his knee before heading back to her
chair and arranging a blanket over her own lap. Alice
smiled to herself. The man seemed to have that effect
on everyone he met.

As they all settled back in their chairs, watching the
sparks spiralling up from their bonfire into the dusky
sky, Alice sipped her hot chocolate and let out a sigh.
She was warm and cosy and incredibly happy. She kept
shooting sideways glances at Jake as he sipped his
drink, his gorgeous face serene in the flickering fire-
light. It seemed like nothing ever ruffled him.

Alice forced herself to look back at the fire. The
only thing that would make this evening any better
would be if she could cosy up with Jake under that
blanket. The couple of feet between them felt like a gulf
- and the unspoken words even harder to bear.

Uh oh, she was going to drive herself potty if she
kept thinking like this. But he'd been about to say
something to her earlier, hadn't he?! Just before they'd
been interrupted, he'd taken her hand. Just for a
second. She was sure he'd finally been about to
mention their kiss. He'd said that he wanted her problems to be his... but... but... what did that mean?

'Erm – time to get the biscuits out?' she said, tearing
her eyes away from Jake's firelit face yet again and
wrestling her way back out of her blanket.

'Absolutely!' said Arthur. 'Can't believe we've waited this long.'

Alice wandered over to the wall where they'd left the large Tupperware box, relishing the cooler air for a moment as it ruffled her hair. She prized the lid off the top of the biscuits, getting a waft of sugary goodness from inside the tub.

'Wow, Nell!' she said. 'These look gorgeous.'

'Thanks,' said Nell. 'Now all I need to know is which ones are your favourites so that I can make them for the knitting night.'

'Ah, the things I'm forced to do in the name of research,' laughed Jake as Alice offered him the box. He promptly helped himself to a small stack consisting of one of each type of biscuit.

After the box had made the rounds and Alice was ensconced back under her blanket, there was complete silence other than the crackling of the fire as they all munched their biscuits and sipped their drinks.

'And?' asked Nell when the silence had gone on for way longer than it should.

'Don't look at me,' said Arthur, licking crumbs off of his fingers.

Alice let out a snort of laughter. She knew where her dad was coming from. The biscuits were all freshly baked and absolutely delicious. There was no way she'd be able to choose between them.

'You're hopeless,' sighed Nell. 'Come on Jake, help a woman out?'

Jake cocked an eyebrow. 'I like this one,' he said, waving the last remnant of a gooey triple chocolate cookie at her.

'That one's your favourite?' asked Nell.

Jake shook his head. 'I didn't say that. I'm not playing favourites here… they're all too good.'

'You lot are useless, seriously. Alice?'

'Alllll of them,' she groaned, taking another bite of a light, lemony biscuit.

'Great,' huffed Nell, her eyes twinkling. 'I come all this way for a decision and you can't even do that. I'm going to have to make all of them for the knitters, aren't I?'

She looked between the three of them and started laughing as she got three enthusiastic nods in return.

'Fine,' she sighed in mock outrage.

'Well,' said Jake, 'if that's the decision made… we can finish the samples off, can't we?'

Nell rolled her eyes. The Tupperware box had ended up on her lap, so she handed it back over to Jake.

'Oi, you,' huffed Arthur, watching Jake closely, 'no hogging the triple chocolate!'

'Or the lemon!' said Alice.

'I'm after the ginger, myself,' said Jake, tearing the lid off again and having an enthusiastic rummage through the contents, helping himself to a selection.

By the time they'd scoffed their way to the bottom of the container and were busy brushing biscuit crumbs off their blankets, darkness had fallen completely and the stars had bloomed in the sky.

Alice shivered slightly and snuggled down a little further into her blanket.

'You know,' sighed Nell, getting to her feet, 'I hate to break up the party, but I'd better be getting home.'

'Are you sure?' said Arthur, leaping to his feet. 'Can't tempt you with a hot chocolate top-up?'

Nell shook her head and smiled. 'Time for me to turn in.'

'In that case, I'll walk you home,' said Arthur. 'Come up to the house for a minute so that I can grab my decent torch!'

Alice watched as her father extended an arm to Nell, and she took it with a grateful smile. They both said goodnight and then pottered away into the shadows.

'Erm,' said Jake, tearing his eyes away from the retreating couple and turning to Alice. 'I know it's none of my business, but... Arthur and Nell?'

Alice smiled at him and shook her head. 'They've been friends for years – ever since I was little. I don't think there's anything more than that between them... but I do wonder if maybe there could be... one day. If I'm honest though, I think dad still misses mum too much, even after all these years.'

Jake nodded and stared into the crackling embers of the fire. Alice gave another involuntary shiver. Blimey, it was getting cold fast now that it was properly dark.

'You okay?' said Jake, turning to her.

Alice nodded. Damn - she hadn't wanted him to notice. The last thing she wanted to happen was for him to decide to call it a night as well.

Jake didn't say anything, but he stood up and shuffled his chair over so that it was right next to hers. Then he grabbed Nell's abandoned blanket and sat down next to Alice, wrapping the warm wool right around both of them.

Alice turned to him. His face was now so close to her own, and their combined body heat mingled under the blanket, taking the chill off the evening. She smiled at him, and Jake smiled back. Neither of them said anything. After waiting all evening to finish the conversation they'd started earlier, suddenly, there didn't seem to be any need to.

'Jake - look!' laughed Alice. A movement out of the corner of her eye caught had her attention. She pointed over at Basil. The little dog had spotted that Arthur's blanket had slithered into a heap on the ground, and he was busy pawing it into a comfy shape. As they watched, Basil circled once, then twice, and then flopped down into the blanket's cosy folds for a much-needed nap.

'Well, he's had a busy afternoon,' chuckled Jake.

Alice grinned at him and nodded. Basil had spent most of the afternoon snuffling around and chasing small, furry things that were busy making their escape from the disturbed undergrowth. He'd had a good sniff at a frog and chewed a slug - though he'd given that up as a bad idea pretty quickly.

Letting out a huge sigh of contentment, without even thinking about what she was doing, Alice let her head drop onto Jake's shoulder as Basil started to snore loudly.

Jake dropped a soft kiss onto her hair and Alice smiled gently into the cosy glow coming from the embers of the fire. Considering how awful the day had seemed earlier - it was ending a lot better than she could have ever dreamed.

CHAPTER 13

'Jake? Lunch!' Alice called, wandering into the visitors' centre and setting the tray she was carrying down on an upturned cardboard box beneath one of the windows.

She straightened up and ran a finger over the beautifully restored sill, smiling as she traced the seam where the old wood joined the new. This had been one of the worst - full of rot - but Jake had painstakingly removed the damaged timber. Then, rather than filling it with something synthetic, he'd managed to fit a large chunk of oak into the hole, shaving and sanding it until it fitted perfectly.

Jake had been spending most of his waking hours working on the visitors' centre and it was coming together beautifully. Now that he'd undone most of the terrible things Warren had inflicted on the old building, it was all starting to feel a lot more positive.

The brick walls inside and out had been repointed, and one by one, the old windows were being brought back to their former glory. Yes - it was taking a great deal of time to do the work properly, but Alice had loved seeing the quality of Jake's work. The man had immense patience as well as pride in his work - without becoming precious and long-winded about the whole process.

It was so very different to how Warren had oper-ated. Her ex could take an entire day just to sand a tiny stretch of wood - not because he was being careful - just because he was lazy and didn't believe in sanding. Frankly, there had been moments when he'd barely looked like he was moving at all. Alice had always been under the impression that there needed to be some actual friction involved in sanding!

That was the thing with Warren, though - he got as little done as was humanly possible before taking a long lunch break. Jake couldn't be more different. He barely ever seemed to stop - to the point where she had to turn up and physically waft coffee and a bite to eat under his nose to tempt him into taking a break.

'Jake! Lunch and coffee!' she called again.

'Hey - sorry!' Jake's face appeared around the door-frame and Alice chuckled at the sight of him. His eyebrows were full of tiny flecks of sawdust.

'Come here,' she said, moving towards him. 'Close your eyes!'

'Blimey Alice,' said Jake, giving her a naughty smile.

'I mean it - unless you want sawdust in your coffee!' she said in a mock-stern voice, crossing her arms until he did as she said.

Stepping forward, Alice gently brushed the sawdust from his face.

'There,' she said. She was about to take a step back when Jake cracked his eyes open and placed a light kiss on her lips.

Alice froze for a moment before wrapping her arms around his waist and kissing him again. She could get used to this! In fact… she already was.

Ever since the evening they'd had the fire, the pair of them had been spending plenty of time together. They'd passed their evenings in the boathouse, patching holes in the old circus tent as best as they could so that it would be ready for the big night.

'Drink your coffee, before it gets cold!' she said, pulling away from him at last.

'Are you and your dad still up for putting the tent up this afternoon?' he asked, gratefully taking the mug from her.

Alice nodded. 'Yep - dad said he'll drive the tractor around so that we've got a bit of extra grunt to get it up.'

Her last three words made Jake start to giggle so hard that he had to put his coffee down again. Alice bit her lip, desperately trying not to join in with him. This happened every single time they talked about the tent. One or other of them would start giggling and that was it for a good half an hour. The words *erecting, getting it up* and even *raising* usually managed to reduce the pair of them into a blubbering, giggling mess. *Raising* was probably the safest - but it still managed to set them off nine times out of ten.

'Is Basil still okay with Arthur?' asked Jake, wiping his eyes and manfully trying to change the subject. 'And vice versa?'

Alice nodded, still laughing. 'Dad's loving the company - and he's plying Basil with biscuits as they go so...'

Jake grinned. 'So he'll be happy as Larry, then. I just don't want him to get in the way.'

'No chance of that - I think dad's in love!' she said, then promptly blushed.

Shit. Why on earth did she have to go and bring up the l-word?!

'I can't believe the first *Knit One Pour One* is tonight!' she said, quickly changing the subject yet again. 'Thank goodness for your tent. Even with you working on this place every hour of the day, it would never have been ready, would it?'

Jake shook his head. 'Afraid not. There was too much of Warren's mess to undo first. But - in theory - it won't be too much longer before you guys can move in here!'

'I'm still a bit worried about the tent though,' she sighed.

'Nah - I reckon it'll be grand. We've patched up all

the holes,' said Jake with a shrug.

'Yeah - it's going to look great, but I think it'll be quite hard to raise it!'

Jake sniggered again.

'Behave!' she laughed.

'You started it!' Jake winked at her.

'Fair point. Anyway - dad said he'd be ready to help in about twenty minutes.'

'Perfect,' said Jake. 'Let's head down there now. I'll eat this on the way!' He grabbed the sandwich she'd made for him and took a huge bite before picking up his mug again and leading the way to the door.

They wandered towards the boathouse in companionable silence, Jake's sandwich and coffee disappearing in record time.

'You're quiet,' he said as they made their way along the flower-strewn path. 'Is everything okay?'

Alice nodded quickly. 'Absolutely,' she laughed. 'Just running lists in my head for later. Do you ever do that?'

Jake let out a hearty laugh and shook his head. 'Can't say that I do. I guess I'm one of those people who just focuses on what I'm doing in the moment – I don't tend to think much beyond what needs doing that day, to be honest.'

'I wish I could be more like that,' said Alice with a sigh. 'I feel a bit like my head's going to explode sometimes.'

'What's it exploding with right now?' asked Jake, eyeing her curiously.

'Whether it's going to rain this evening. And if it does, will the tent be waterproof? And what to do if it isn't...'

'Wow,' laughed Jake, holding his hands up.

Alice saw him peep up at the forget-me-not blue sky.

'I know,' she said, 'sorry, I'm being an idiot.'

Jake shook his head. 'No, you're not. And for the record – you never have to apologise for being you because... well, I like you exactly the way you are – *listing* quirks and all!'

Alice couldn't help but beam at Jake as he reached out, took her hand and linked his fingers with hers.

'I like you just as you are too,' she said, cringing slightly as her voice came out sounding all young and shy. She felt him give her fingers a squeeze before he started swinging their hands between them like they were a pair of six-year-olds.

'Then all's well, eh?' he said. 'And as for your list... I've already gathered a whole load of buckets, watering cans and containers from around the place... just in case!'

Alice felt the tension in her shoulders loosen again. The pair of them couldn't be any more different – and yet Jake had a way of just making life seem... right.

They rounded the bend in the path and the boathouse came into view. Alice couldn't believe how quickly she'd come to think of it as "Jake's place". As they approached, she did her best to ignore the bits of van engine that seemed to be littered everywhere. She had no clue if Jake was getting anywhere with his repairs, and if she was being honest, she didn't want to ask him outright.

'I guess we'd better open both doors,' said Jake, striding forward and hauling one open as Alice made a move to help with the other. 'Should make it easier to get the tent out again!'

Alice nodded as she kicked an old house brick in front of her door to hold it open. There were bits of van lying around inside too, and she sighed. She knew that as soon as the van was running again, there was a very real chance that Jake would leave. There hadn't been any promises between them, after all. Maybe their relationship – or whatever you wanted to call this wonderful thing that had started to bloom between them – was as temporary as the circus tent.

She turned and picked her way through the various bits of unidentified engine. Surely, if so much of the vehicle's innards were in here rather than inside the van, they would still have a decent bit of time together before Jake left? Alice's heart lightened at the thought.

'I'll shift those bits of engine out of the way of the door!' said Jake, catching her staring at them.

'Brill,' said Alice. 'I still can't believe how heavy that tent is! Dad said he'll drive up to the door with the tractor so we can just heave it straight on.'

'That's a relief,' laughed Jake as he scooted a bunch of van parts that were sitting on a piece of old rug out of the way. 'The thing's a beast when it comes to shifting it around!'

'I'd like to think it's because of all the extra bits we've sewn in!' she laughed.

Jake shook his head and chuckled. 'Don't reckon a few pieces of shower curtain are going to make it much heavier than it already was.'

Alice stared down at the tent. They'd patched all the holes they could find using a mixture of old sails, a second-hand shower curtain and even an old coat of her dad's that was well past its best. It had been a bit of a struggle sneaking it out of the house without Arthur noticing, but it had been the perfect thing to patch up one of the larger tears.

Alice couldn't wait to see it when it was up and rigged. It would certainly be unique!

'Where are the pegs?' said Alice, looking around for the new stakes the pair of them had cut from the hazel stands at the far edge of one of the fields further along the river. They'd chopped them to size and sharpened them so that they would be easy to hammer into the newly-cleared ground. The last thing Alice wanted was for the tent to fly off in the middle of the festivities.

'Over there in that old washing basket!' said Jake, pointing at an old, faded yellow thing that was tucked away on one of the shelves at the back.

'Perfect,' she said, heading over and picking it up. 'Now all we've got to do is get it up and decorate it.'

Jake promptly started to giggle.

'What?' she demanded.

'Get. It. Up!' howled Jake, almost dropping the heavy bit of engine he was doing his best to cart out of the way.

Alice rolled her eyes and went over to help him. She didn't want to admit it, but she was secretly dreading trying to get the tent sited. What if it went wrong? Then she'd be left with nowhere for their guests... that's if there were any guests... what if none of them turned up?

'Alice? You've zoned out on me again,' laughed Jake.

'Sorry. I'm back!' she shot him a grin.

'Stop worrying! Now we've fixed all those holes, the rest will be a doddle - especially with your dad's help!'

He turned to peer out through the double doors. Alice followed his gaze and sure enough, she could hear the noisy tractor engine revving up in the distance.

'Here you go!' said Jake, handing Alice the mallet. She took it and thumped the last of their hand-made pegs into the ground, securing the final guy rope neatly and making sure that the massive tent wouldn't fall over.

'Doesn't it look amazing?' said Alice as she peered up at the patched stripes from her crouching position next to the peg.

'It really does!' came Nell's voice from behind her.

Nell had rocked up just in time to join their raising

party, and with her help as well as Jake, her dad, the tractor and Basil - it had gone without a hitch.

'Here,' laughed Jake, holding out his and for Alice and then hauling her back up to her feet.

'Ta,' said Alice, blushing slightly as she bumped into him. Jake wrapped his arms around her rather than letting her go.

'Good work team!' said Arthur, as he reappeared from taking the tractor back around to the barn.

Thank heavens for the tractor! Alice wasn't quite sure how they would have managed without it keeping the heavy, central pole safely upright while they all ran around, securing the ropes. But it was done now – thank goodness. She let herself relax a little in Jake's embrace.

'Ah... that's the tent well and truly christened then!' Arthur added. He pointed at Basil, who'd just done a full round of inspection of the wooden pegs, chosen his favourite and cocked his leg.

Alice let out a surprised laugh. 'Well, at least he approves of it!'

'Honestly Basil,' muttered Jake, 'I seriously cannot take you anywhere, can I?'

'Isn't that your old coat, Arthur?' Nell asked as her eyes landed on the large patch.

'Nell!' said Jake, quickly cutting in and patting her on the arm, 'why don't you and Arthur have a look inside?'

Alice smiled at him gratefully. He was clearly doing

his best to distract her and Arthur before the latter clocked what Nell had just spotted.

Nell looked surprised and then nodded with a smile. All four of them trouped inside the tent for a proper look, closely followed by Basil.

As soon as Alice stepped through the entrance flap, all her worries about the evening ahead disappeared. It looked amazing in here – and that was before she'd had the chance to bring in the chairs, tables and various decorations she had planned.

'Well done, you two!' said Arthur, looking around, wide-eyed.

'Thanks dad,' laughed Alice, her delight bubbling over. 'It's all down to Jake really!'

'It's magical in here,' said Nell, nodding her agreement.

'It is!' agreed Arthur, nodding.

Alice glanced at her father and smiled. Ever since Jake had arrived at the vineyard, her dad's crusty, grumpy edge seemed to have worn away. She couldn't remember a time when she'd had so much fun working alongside him, and it made her even more excited for their future here together.

'Well,' said Nell, 'I think this calls for some apple crumble cookies and a cuppa, don't you?'

Alice nodded. 'Sounds just about perfect to me.'

'Hey,' said Arthur as they made their way back towards the entrance flap. 'You know… I think you're right. That *is* my coat!'

CHAPTER 14

*A*lice reached up and flipped one of the bunting flags over so that it hung straight, and then gave a little nod of satisfaction. Everything was ready. The strings of lights that Jake had found in the boathouse were looped overhead. She'd washed and ironed the brightly coloured vintage bunting, and it looked incredible against the stripes and patches of the old circus tent.

Weirdly, the bits of shower curtain, sailcloth and old coat the pair of them had used to patch the old thing up added to its charm rather than making it look shabby.

Jake and her father had helped her to move the newly-painted and restored wooden chairs up from the boathouse, and they were now set out in a circle. They looked great. Okay, well... maybe *great* was pushing it a tiny bit... but they looked lovely and colourful at least.

There were a few tables dotted around and she'd covered them with striped linen table clothes. Nell had helped her to set out plates heaped with huge piles of biscuits, and there was plenty of tea and coffee ready to go for anyone who didn't want wine.

The wine itself was lined up on a little side table for anyone who fancied a taste test... you never knew when someone might fancy treating themselves to a bottle or six.

Alice did a final, mini-circuit of the space. There was nothing more that she could do now, except hope against hope that people would turn up. She knew what the village could be like when the rumour mill got going – and she couldn't help but worry about what damage Warren might have done with his fake news. One thing was for sure though – it was going to be pretty lonely if no one appeared... and the three of them would be living on biscuits for the foreseeable future!

Just as her nerves were starting to get the better of her, Alice heard footsteps approaching outside. Taking a deep breath, she made her way towards the entrance only to find Lionel Barclay making his way towards her.

'I can't believe you came all the way up from Seabury!' squealed Alice, running to him and throwing her arms around him.

Lionel returned the hug and gave her a bristly kiss on the cheek. He'd known her since she was a baby, and Alice thought of him a bit like an honorary grandad.

'I wouldn't miss it for the world!' he said. 'I needed to pick up some more wine for the hotel anyway, but I've been looking forward to meeting some other knitters for ages. We don't have anything like this in Seabury.'

'Well, fingers crossed some more people will come - otherwise, it'll be just the pair of us... and I still don't know how to knit.'

Lionel laughed. 'Don't give me that rubbish, young lady - I taught you how to cast on when you were six.'

'And I never got any further!' said Alice, beaming at him.

'Well, we'll soon rectify that,' said Lionel, patting the squashy tote bag he had slung over his shoulder. 'I've got enough wool and needles in here to kit out the entire village if they turn up. I didn't know if you had any spares, and as I had more than enough lying around, I thought I'd bring some along in case anyone wanted a go but didn't have the kit!'

'That's amazing,' said Alice, 'thank you so much.'

'Not a problem! I must say I rather love your choice of venue for the evening. I had my reservations when your dad mentioned it in his last phone call, but this is much better than I expected! Very shabby chic!'

'Thanks Lionel. I'm chuffed at how it's turned out. Though, I have to admit that I've been having kittens about it for days. Anyway – never mind all that!' said

Alice, quickly, 'tell me everything – you bought a *hotel?!*'

'Not *a* hotel – *my* hotel,' said Lionel, his eyes sparkling. 'I've finally bought my home... and the restaurant is already doing amazing things thanks to my great-niece. You know, you'll have to come and visit soon – I think you and Hattie would get on a treat.'

'I'd love that – thanks!' said Alice.

'Come and stay for a night or two – I can use you as a guinea pig when we've finished doing up the rooms. Then you can meet Hattie and test out her delicious food. Speaking of which...' his eyes drifted over to the towering piles of biscuits.

'Help yourself!' laughed Alice. 'Nell made enough for a month's supply!'

'Can I try more than one?' said Lionel, the excitement on his face making him look like a little boy.

'As many as you can manage,' said Alice. She watched as Lionel grabbed one of the plates and started to load it with one of each of the flavours. Well – that had to be a good sign!

'Lionel, old boy!'

Alice turned and promptly let out a surprised gasp. Her father had just entered the tent behind Nell. Lionel turned to greet his old friend and he did a double-take too.

'Arthur! I barely recognised you!' he said, beaming and hurrying over to shake her dad's hand.

'Dad – you look incredible,' said Alice, eyeballing her father's new haircut and clean sweater in surprise.

'I second that!' said Lionel. 'If only I could get a haircut that took ten years off me!'

Arthur chuckled. 'Well, you'll have to ask our Nell here.'

'Nell?' said Alice in surprise. 'You cut dad's hair for him?'

Nell nodded, her eyes twinkling. 'I did it with the kitchen scissors.'

'And I've still got both my ears,' said Arthur, causing Nell to swat him on the arm.

'It looks wonderful, Nell,' said Alice.

'It's not all that,' said Nell, 'but it's certainly an improvement. And he barely grumbled about it at all, which was a surprise - I thought he'd be a lot worse!'

Alice grinned at her. She didn't say anything but frankly, Nell had basically just worked a miracle. It was enough that her dad had let Nell cut his hair, but persuading him to change out of his favourite, holey green jumper for the occasion was something else entirely.

Alice couldn't help but feel chuffed that the pair of them were getting along so well – especially considering how long Nell had had a thing for her father.

'So, how many are we expecting this evening?' asked Arthur, helping himself to a biscuit from Lionel's heaped plate.

Alice shrugged. 'I have absolutely no idea. We could

be packed... we could be empty... or we might land somewhere in between. It's hard to tell after... well...'

'Don't mention that idiot this evening,' said her father. 'Even if it's just us lot, we'll have fun, okay?'

Alice smiled at him gratefully. 'Have you seen Jake?'

Arthur shook his head. 'I'm sure he'll be here. He's probably tinkering about with that old van of his.'

Alice nodded, her heart sinking slightly. Sure, the innards of the van might be strewn around the floor of the boathouse awaiting some TLC, but she'd seen how fast Jake could make things happen when he put his mind to it. She hated the idea of him leaving. He'd become such a huge part of their life here at the vineyard. It was already becoming hard to imagine the place without him. In fact, she didn't want to.

'Don't you have a fashion designer or something living around here somewhere?' asked Lionel with interest.

Alice nodded, forcing a smile back onto her face. 'Patricia Woodley. She's got the house down by Bamton Ford. She's actually a knitting pattern designer. Incredible knitter, apparently. She's really lovely, but I don't expect her to show up – it's not like she needs any tips!'

'You never know,' said Lionel, 'people do love a bit of company with their craft...'

'And wine!' said Arthur, raising his newly poured glass of red.

. . .

After that, there wasn't very much time to stand around and chat – because, against all odds, the tent began to fill up fast. Marjorie from the village arrived with a bag of scarves. Much to Alice's amusement, she set up camp on one of the brightly painted chairs and merrily began to unravel them, turning them back into balls of wool as she chatted away to Lionel, who was working on a complicated-looking fisherman's jumper.

Nell and her father had sat down together and she was gently trying to teach him to cast on. There was a lot of giggling coming from their direction, and her dad had to be cut out of the middle of the mess a couple of times before he got into the swing of things.

Next came Gloria and a couple of gents – one she recognised as the guy who ran the ferry across the river in the summer.

'Alice, love!' said Gloria with a wide smile. 'This is James.'

'Hi!' said Alice, shaking his rough hand. 'I recognise you from the ferry!'

'That's right,' he said with a smile. 'It's a bit early in the year to be out there just yet though and the boat's up on the bank for a bit of maintenance. Won't be long before she's back in the water.'

Alice smiled at him, thinking that she'd have to introduce him to Jake. Something told her the pair of them would probably bond over all things oily and engine-related… if Jake ever turned up, that was.

For a second, her heart sank. Perhaps he wasn't

coming. She realised, with a horrible twist in her stomach, that she hadn't actually invited him... she'd just assumed he'd turn up. But how was the poor bloke meant to know that he was invited - by osmosis?

She smiled and nodded as even more villagers appeared, and did her best to keep herself distracted by making sure that everyone knew they were welcome to wine, tea, coffee and biscuits. James asked her dad lots of questions about the vineyard while sipping on a glass of their most expensive red wine. He then proceeded to delight Arthur by declaring it the most delicious thing he'd ever tasted and ordered a whole case as a gift for his dad.

The tent was now heaving and the burble of relaxed conversation was almost deafening. Everyone had settled down to some knitting and a good gossip session.

Alice turned to the door, hoping against hope that Jake might appear, and had trouble stopping herself from squealing. Because there he was, along with Patricia – their resident knitting expert. Alice couldn't believe she'd come, and she was having a hard time deciding who she was more excited to see – her or Jake!

'I'm sorry I'm late!' said Patricia, coming over to her.

'You're not at all – help yourself – there's tea, coffee, wine, biscuits...'

'Nell's biscuits?' said Patricia, her eyes lighting up.

Alice nodded. 'Mountains of them.'

'I think I might have died and gone to heaven,' laughed Patricia.

'Help yourself!' said Alice, grinning at her.

'Hello you,' said Jake, leaning in to nudge her arm as a stuffed carrier bag swung from his fingers.

'Hi! I didn't know if you were going to turn up!'

'Give over,' laughed Jake, 'I wouldn't have missed it for the world. I just wanted to move all those engine bits back inside in case it rained… and now look at it out there… clear as anything.'

'And after you gathered all those buckets in case of drips too,' she laughed. They both glanced under one of the tables where their stack of emergency-drip-buckets were discreetly tucked away.

'Better have them and not need them,' said Jake.

'True. So, what's in the bag?' said Alice.

Jake plunged his hand inside and drew out a large piece of knitting on a pair of chunky wooden needles.

'You knit?!' said Alice, looking at the half-finished cardigan in surprise.

'I started this when I was up on Crumcarey Island… but that was months ago. I never seem to get the chance or the time to finish the thing,' he sighed.

'Impressive,' said Alice.

Jake shrugged. 'Hardly! It's my first attempt – and it's a bit of a mess. The tension is all over the gaff and there's the odd hole too…'

As Alice watched him, her heart melted even

further. Discovering that there was at least one thing that Jake wasn't ridiculously good at was strangely reassuring.

'Anyway,' said Jake, tearing his eyes away from the half-finished project in his hands, 'I don't intend to wear it. I'll probably just turn it into a net to catch some fish or something.'

'Fish, huh?' laughed Alice.

'Or something!' said Jake, with a grin. 'It'll be nice to get it finished off though. It gave me something to do in the evenings... until recently, of course!' He wiggled his eyebrows at her.

Alice walloped him on the arm. She just hoped the blush that had just lit up her cheeks would disappear before anyone noticed that she was doing a good impression of a roasting tomato.

'Oi,' she muttered, making Jake snigger before he leaned in and kissed her lightly.

Huh. So much for going unnoticed!

CHAPTER 15

*A*lice let out a ginormous yawn and stared around the tent which was – *finally* - empty. As the daylight had begun to fade, it became very clear that none of their guests were ready to head home any time soon. So, her father had brought in several old oil lamps to light the space. The tent looked so cosy in their flickering glow.

It was now well past ten o'clock, and even though she was sad it was over, Alice was secretly glad that everyone had finally called it a night. It had been a fantastic evening, but she felt like she was asleep on her feet.

The first-ever *Knit One Pour One* really couldn't have gone better. There had been plenty of gossip, a great deal of biscuit eating... and even some actual knitting. A couple of scarves had progressed by an inch or two – though several people had clearly found the sight of Marjorie merrily unpicking a couple of sweaters a tad dispiriting. Though, as Nell had whispered to her at one point – at least they didn't have to eat Marjorie's cake with its hedgerow ingredients too!

Unfortunately, Alice wasn't quite so sure they'd get away with that a second time. Marjorie had promised on her way home that she'd be sure to "pull her weight with the catering" next time.

That being said, Gloria had also loudly offered to help out next time, promising to make sandwiches. This had sparked a lively debate about fillings and whether the bread should be white or wholemeal, and whether the crusts should be cut off or not. The eventual outcome had been that everyone agreed that perhaps biscuits were a better bet... leaving Gloria's nose well and truly out of joint. Not that it lasted long. Gloria was far too fond of gossip and had had too much wine to stay stroppy for more than about thirty seconds.

Alice grinned to herself as she gathered together the empty biscuit plates. There had practically been a stampede towards the end of the evening when people had realised that there were some of their favourites left. More than one person had gone home with their pockets full of a little snack for the road.

'Well, Alice my girl, that's what I call a resounding success.'

Arthur smiled at her warmly as he reappeared in

the tent. He'd just taken Lionel up to the house and settled him into one of their guest rooms for the night.

'It went well, didn't it?' said Alice, returning his smile gratefully.

'*Well?* I should say so! Considering that not very long ago it looked like we'd have to call the whole thing off - I'd say it was a complete triumph! By the way, Lionel ordered far more wine than I was expecting - and we sold a whole load of bottles to the others too.'

'We did?' said Alice. 'That's brilliant. I wasn't sure if that part of the plan was going to work or not!' She had to admit, she'd got so caught up in the knitting lesson she was getting from Lionel, that she hadn't really clocked what was happening with the wine sales.

'You know, I enjoyed the knitting part more than I thought I would. Nell taught me how to cast on and cast off. Just think - me... knitting!' he said, looking rather pleased with himself. 'And everyone was very nice about my new haircut even though it's a bit wonky at the back.' He cast a furtive glance over his shoulder and then added in a whisper, 'don't tell Nell I said that though!'

Alice laughed. 'I'm so glad you had a good time. And you *do* look very dapper!'

'Thanks love! Everything turned out far better than I could have hoped, and I'll be the first to admit that you were right all along.'

'What - about the biscuits?' said Alice, shaking crumbs off of one of the tablecloths.

'No, you daft girl. About the fact that it was a good idea to invite everyone back here. It's time this community got together again. It's a small one after all... who'd have thought that all it would take was a tent and a few biscuits to get them talking to each other?!'

'That and a bit of knitting... and alcohol!' she laughed.

Arthur sighed. 'I should have done this years ago, shouldn't I?'

Alice shook her head. 'Dad - the community prob-ably wouldn't even exist if you'd sold off the vineyard and it had all been turned into holiday homes. Maybe it's a good thing that you protected the place from the outside world for a little while.'

'Maybe,' sighed Arthur.

'You've got to admit,' she said with a smile, 'it was a lot of fun getting everyone together tonight.'

'A *lot* of fun,' said Arthur, 'and I'm already looking forward to the next one!'

Alice beamed at him. 'Thanks dad.'

'I know I've said this before, but your mother would be very proud of you - for making me see that it's okay to let other people in again. I realise it's taken me a year... or ten... to actually listen to you! But take Jake, for example. What a breath of fresh air he's turned out to be!'

Alice nodded, trying to keep her smile natural and not

looking too much like she'd just lost the plot. The mere mention of Jake made her heart skip and heat flooded her face. The man in question was busy helping Nell ferry various bits and pieces across to the farmhouse. If it had been left up to Alice, she would have waited until morning to tidy everything up, but Nell had insisted.

'To think,' said Arthur, 'Jake was just a trespasser to start with!'

'Yep. And if it wasn't for the fact that Basil had been snoring when I found the van down by the river, I'd have probably just told them to clear off there and then!'

'You know, I'll be sorry to see him leave,' said Arthur, looking at her intently. 'He's the first one of your boyfriends that I've actually approved of, you know.'

Alice's jaw dropped. She quickly checked over her shoulder but thankfully Jake was nowhere to be seen.

'I, erm… I'm not sure about *boyfriend,*' she muttered. 'Anyway, I wasn't sure you'd noticed that anything was going on between us.'

'Oh please,' laughed Arthur, finding half a lemon biscuit in one of the remaining Tupperware boxes and stuffing it in his mouth with relish. 'I wasn't born yesterday!' he added when he'd swallowed the morsel. 'Even before you started canoodling in front of the whole village earlier on - it was pretty obvious some-thing was going on between you.'

'Really?' said Alice, shifting awkwardly as her dad grinned at her.

'Really!' laughed Arthur. 'I'm happy for you. He's a lovely lad - I'm just sorry he's planning on leaving.'

Alice swallowed hard. It always led back to that eventually, didn't it? She'd been trying so hard not to think too much about Jake leaving – but of course, that's what was going to happen – and probably pretty soon too.

Alice swallowed the lump that had risen in her throat. She didn't want to think about it - not when it could put a dampener on such a brilliant evening.

These last few weeks had been some of the best and busiest she could remember. She'd loved hanging out with Jake - spending busy days with him as they worked together to get the visitors' centre finished followed by long, lovely evenings down at the boathouse. Of course - she'd been busy before, but this was different. This was about moving the whole vine-yard forward rather than just firefighting disasters.

Somehow, Jake had helped them to shift out of the past. Together, they'd started to make things better. Mend them. Heal them. No - there was no way she'd have been able to do any of this without Jake. She thought of all the little things that he'd thrown his time, energy and passion into - like her dad's boat. Like this tent. Like the beautifully restored wood in the visitors' centre.

Alice wouldn't have known where to start. Warren

certainly wouldn't have had a clue either - he just wanted to knock things down, cover them over and make a profit from them. But Jake just didn't think like that. Suddenly, Alice couldn't bear the idea of the place without him. What would she do when Jake was gone?

CHAPTER 16

'*A*lice, love?'

Alice followed her father's call into the kitchen.

'Morning dad! Everything okay?'

She did her best not to look too shifty. Ever since *Knit One Pour One* a few nights ago, she'd been sneaking out of the farmhouse after they'd all gone to bed and spending the nights with Jake down in the boathouse.

Much to Jake's intense amusement, she'd also been sneaking back *into* the farmhouse using her trusty old teenage route up the apple tree and through her bedroom window. It didn't matter that her father already knew that she and Jake were an item… Alice just wasn't quite ready for him to know that it had reached that point!

'I'm fine, thanks,' grinned Arthur, pouring her a cup

of coffee from the cafetière and handing it to her. 'I've got a phone message I need to give you. I've got to say though, I'm glad to see you're still in one piece after another morning of acrobatics!'

Alice stared at her father in horror, but Arthur was too busy chuckling at her to notice her discomfort.

'Did Jake blab on me?!' she demanded in horror.

Arthur shook his head. 'As if he'd do something like that!'

'Then how…?'

'Madam – I lone-parented you as a teenager. Don't think I don't know the signs when you're busy scaling that tree… though I have to say, it's been a very long time since you've pulled that particular trick!'

Arthur paused and eyed Alice sternly. She felt like parts of her universe were shifting. Her dad *knew* that she'd disappeared via the window all the way through her teenage rebellious phase?!

'Don't look like that!' laughed Arthur. 'I'm guessing you're enjoying the danger element… but just so you know, you're welcome to use the door instead.'

'Erm… okay?' said Alice, totally mortified. 'And… and you're really okay with everything?'

Arthur looked at her in amusement, cocking his head to one side. 'For one thing, I'd say that you're probably old enough to make those decisions for your-self by now. And for another thing, I've already had words with Jake!'

'Words?' Alice repeated in a faint voice.

'Words. Me and Lionel, actually. We told him that if he ever hurt you, then he'd have both of us to answer to.'

Alice bit her lip. She was caught somewhere between the complete horror of the situation and wanting to laugh at the thought of Lionel and her father cornering Jake. Poor guy!

'Anyway, as I said, I like Jake. Very straightforward kind of bloke.'

'And… erm… what did he say?' she asked, not sure she really wanted to know.

'That's for me to know and you to find out,' chuckled Arthur.

'Daaaaad,' she whined.

'And there's another thing you haven't done since you were a teenager!' he laughed. 'Anyway, drink your coffee and let me give you this message before I forget all about it.'

Alice sipped her coffee in moody silence and watched him pick up a scrap of paper from beside their old fashioned landline telephone.

'Right – it's from the mechanic over at Bamton Motors calling for Jake about the van. He said that he can't come and see it this afternoon – but he'll be over first thing tomorrow morning instead.'

Alice nodded, her heart sinking. That meant the van would be mended and Jake would be gone. She was certain of it. Now that he'd almost finished with the visitors' centre, there would be nothing to keep him here. Give it a couple more days and he'd just be waiting on the electricians and the plumber to turn up... and she could oversee that.

Jake's work was almost finished, and he'd done a spectacular job. It looked like she'd always imagined it - but somehow even better because it had all been done with so much love.

'You happy to let him know?' said Arthur.

Alice looked up and caught his eye. The understanding she saw there nearly reduced her to tears, and she quickly swallowed down the wave of emotion and nodded. 'I'll go find him,' she said.

Alice hurried off, not really wanting her dad to start comforting her. She knew he'd clocked exactly what she was thinking, but right now, she didn't want him to say it out loud - that would just make it all too real.

She wasn't sure whether Jake would still be down at the boathouse, or if he'd already be working on the finishing touches in the visitors' centre. She made an executive decision to head there first... even if he wasn't there, it'd give her the chance to calm down a bit. She didn't want to offload her current neediness onto the poor man – after all, he hadn't promised her anything.

Alice let herself out through the back door of the farmhouse and headed around the corner. The unusable pile of materials that Warren had ordered were long-gone. Jake and her father had loaded it all up into his Land Rover and driven it around to the workshop, where it was now stacked neatly. As Jake had said, they'd already paid for it, and it was bound to come in useful somewhere around the place as they slowly worked to do up the various outbuildings.

Now that they'd made a start, Arthur was full of plans for improvements. Ideas on how to make the most of some of the spaces that had been neglected for so long were coming thick and fast. That was yet another thing she had to be thankful to Jake for.

Opening the door into the visitors' centre, Alice took in a long deep breath, inhaling the warm scent of fresh paint and wood shavings.

'Hello?' she called. 'Jake, you in here?'

Total silence. As she expected.

Alice let her shoulders drop. She'd have to head back down to the boathouse to find Jake – but that was okay, it'd give her the chance to get a smile back on her face before she saw him. After all, she had plenty to be cheerful about. This place, for example. It was nearly ready to receive its first guests, and it was just gorgeous.

She wandered through the space and let herself out the other side, where Jake's circus tent still stood proudly on the newly cleared patch of ground. It just seemed to fit, somehow. She knew they'd have to take it down before too long so that it could be all packed up for Jake to take away with him. But for now, she loved seeing it there – it was a gorgeous reminder of a perfect evening.

Knit One Pour One had been such a triumph that she'd agreed to host another one in just a week's time. All the knitters had said that they'd be bringing their friends so it should be another busy night.

There was a slim chance that the plumbing and electrics might be in place in the visitors' centre by then. In a way though, Alice really wanted to hold it in the tent one more time... because at least that would mean Jake was still at the vineyard with them.

Letting out a sigh, she pushed aside the flap and peeked in. All was well in there, with everything stacked up neatly ready to be moved - or pressed into service again.

At least she was sure of one thing was certain, the guests at the next *Knit One Pour One* would be treated to Nell's amazing biscuits again! They'd been such a highlight and Nell had already ordered in more ingredients.

Alice stepped back, dropping the canvas flap as she turned to make her way slowly down towards the boathouse. The weather wasn't quite as nice today – the grey clouds had crowded out the beautiful blue sky and there was a bit of a chill in the air. She let out a dark laugh as she considered how much the weather echoed how she was feeling right now.

'Get a grip, Alice!' she muttered to herself. There was no way she wanted to spoil her last few days with Jake by being sad and moody.

She picked up her pace, striding down the path as

she stared at the frothy swathes of wildflowers swaying in the chilly breeze. It might be heading towards early summer, but the weather definitely hadn't got the memo this morning!

She rounded the corner and broke into a grin as she was greeted by Basil's smiling face.

'Hello boy!' she laughed.

Basil wagged his tail and trotted up to her, sniffing her trainers and then leaning his head against her leg, demanding a tickle. Alice felt her eyes prickle as she bent low and stroked the dog's nose. It wasn't just Jake she was going to miss, was it?!

Pull yourself together, Alice!

'Come on, boy!' she said to her four-legged welcoming committee, 'let's go and find your dad and give him this message.'

Basil gave her hand a lick and then turned to lead the way down the path, glancing over his shoulder every few meters to check that she was still following.

When Jake came into view, Basil sped up into a gallop to meet him, but Alice slowed again. He was busy in front of the boathouse. It looked like he was taking everything out of the back of his van. He was clearly getting himself organised for his next adventure, and Alice felt her heart plummet.

'Hello you!' said Jake, sensing her and turning with a smile. 'I wondered where Basil had got to!'

'Welcoming committee!' said Alice, forcing a smile onto her face.

'I wasn't expecting to see you down here again so soon. Everything alright?' asked Jake, taking two plastic water carriers from the back of the van and placing them on the gravel.

Alice nodded. 'Dad's just given me a phone message for you. The mechanic over at Bamton Motors can't come today, but he'll be here tomorrow morning.'

Jake beamed. 'Brilliant!' he said. 'Thanks for that.'

Alice waited for him to fill her in, but when he hopped into the back of the van without saying anything else, she figured that it was going to be up to her to broach the subject.

'So, erm...' how on earth was she going to ask this without sounding like a clingy, needy pain in the rear? 'So... I guess you must be getting ready to move on then?'

Alice winced. Not needy, but her voice was definitely higher than normal. Quivery. Full of the emotion that had been building up inside her.

Jake's face reappeared and he smiled at her. 'You know, there's something we need to talk about,' he said, hopping down from the van again, empty-handed.

Alice felt her heart sink. She knew what he was about to say, and she wasn't sure she could handle hearing it after all. It was obvious that Jake was going back on the road. There would be no telling if he'd ever come back this way again, or if she'd ever hear from him again come to that. He was a nomad. He'd made her no promises... and after all, it wasn't as though they could have a long-distance relationship, was it?

'I know it's only ever been temporary... this thing between us,' said Alice, forcing the words out. 'I know we never-'

'You've got it backwards,' laughed Jake, shaking his head as he cut across her, coming to stand just in front of her.

'But the van-'

'They're not coming over to fix it for me – just to have a look at it to maybe buy it from me.'

'Buy it?' said Alice, shaking her head in confusion.

'Yes – I'm going to sell it. I wanted to ask you something. I was wondering... if I could stay?'

Alice stared at him, her mouth slightly open in surprise.

'Stay?'

Jake nodded. 'Yes – maybe in the boathouse? With you?'

Basil looked up at her and then went to sit on Jake's feet.

'And Basil!' he said, his lips flickering into a smile as he glanced down at the dog.

'But... what about your travelling?' said Alice, not really sure she could believe that this was happening.

'I feel like... like I've found my home,' said Jake with a little shrug. 'With people I love. I've found you...'

He stepped forward, dodging around Basil to take

Alice's hand. Basil promptly switched allegiances and leaned on Alice's leg instead.

'I mean – I know I appeared out of nowhere… and it all depends on whether you *want* me around of course.'

Alice continued to stare at him. The only things keeping her anchored and making this feel real were Basil's solid weight against her leg and Jake's work-roughened hand in hers. She didn't want him to let go – if he did, she might just float away.

Alice saw Jake swallow and felt bad that her protracted silence was clearly making him nervous… but she simply couldn't get the words out.

'Alice… I don't really have any money – and if I'm honest, that's not likely to change. But I've been in love with you since the first day we met. I didn't want to say anything because… well… I had to be sure. I've never felt like this before. I've been on the road for most of my adult life and it's a big step to settle down.'

Alice nodded, biting her lip. She was almost in tears now and was having to blink them back furiously. She still couldn't say anything, though.

'I want to, Alice. I want to settle down with you. Can I stay?'

It was exactly what she'd wanted to hear, and maybe that's why she was having such a hard time believing that Jake was standing in front of her, saying these words.

She nodded again, finally finding her voice. 'Of

course you can stay,' she said, her words laced with unshed tears. 'I want you to stay more than anything.'

She felt Jake's fingers tighten around hers as he stared down at her.

'The boathouse might need a bit of work before we can move in there full time,' she said, 'but maybe... maybe we can do it together? Just the two of us?'

Jake nodded, his eyes sparkling as he leaned down to kiss her. Before he managed to make contact, Alice pulled away as she felt the nudge of a cold, wet nose on her calf. She glanced down and met Basil's eyes staring indignantly back at her. The little dog let out a soft *wuff!*

Jake laughed and Alice grinned.

'Sorry lad,' she said, 'of course I meant you too. Just the *three* of us.'

She looked back up at Jake and he nodded, before leaning in to kiss her again.

Just the three of them - because they were already a family.

THE END

ALSO BY BETH RAIN

Little Bamton Series:

Little Bamton: The Complete Series Collection: Books 1 - 5

Individual titles:

Christmas Lights and Snowball Fights (Little Bamton Book 1)

Spring Flowers and April Showers (Little Bamton Book 2)

Summer Nights and Pillow Fights (Little Bamton Book 3)

Autumn Cuddles and Muddy Puddles (Little Bamton Book 4)

Christmas Flings and Wedding Rings (Little Bamton Book 5)

Upper Bamton Series:

A New Arrival in Upper Bamton (Upper Bamton Book 1)

Rainy Days in Upper Bamton (Upper Bamton Book 2)

Hidden Treasures in Upper Bamton (Upper Bamton Book 3)

Time Flies By in Upper Bamton (Upper Bamton Book 4)

Standalone Books:

Christmas on Crumcarey

Seabury Series:

Welcome to Seabury (Seabury Book 1)

Trouble in Seabury (Seabury Book 2)

Christmas in Seabury (Seabury Book 3)

Sandwiches in Seabury (Seabury Book 4)

Secrets in Seabury (Seabury Book 5)

Surprises in Seabury (Seabury Book 6)

Dreams and Ice Creams in Seabury (Seabury Book 7)

Mistakes and Heartbreaks in Seabury (Seabury Book 8)

Laughter and Happy Ever After in Seabury (Seabury Book 9)

Seabury Series Collections:

Kate's Story: Books 1 - 3

Hattie's Story: Books 4 - 6

Writing as Bea Fox:

What's a Girl To Do? The Complete Series

Individual titles:

The Holiday: What's a Girl To Do? (Book 1)

The Wedding: What's a Girl To Do? (Book 2)

The Lookalike: What's a Girl To Do? (Book 3)

The Reunion: What's a Girl To Do? (Book 4)

At Christmas: What's a Girl To Do? (Book 5)

ABOUT THE AUTHOR

Beth Rain has always wanted to be a writer and has been penning adventures for characters ever since she learned to stare into the middle-distance and daydream.

She currently lives in the (sometimes) sunny South West, and it is a dream come true to spend her days hanging out with Bob – her trusty laptop – scoffing crisps and chocolate while dreaming up swoony love stories for all her imaginary friends.

Beth's writing will always deliver on the happy-ever-afters, so if you need cosy… you're in safe hands!

Visit www.bethrain.com for all the bookish goodness and keep up with all Beth's news by joining her monthly newsletter!

facebook.com/BethRainBooks
twitter.com/bethrainauthor
instagram.com/bethrainauthor

Printed in Great Britain
by Amazon